EPIGRAPH

"The better I get to know men, the more I find myself loving dogs."

Charles De Gaulle

K-9 VIPER

THE VETERAN'S STORY (K-9 HEROES, BOOK 3)

RADA JONES

Illustrated by
MARIAN JOSTEN

APOLODOR

APOLODOR PUBLISHING

K-9 VIPER

1

The day Butter got shot, I lost a piece of my soul.

We, dogs, often feel things before they happen, but I didn't see that one coming. That day looked just like any other day at our base in Kandahar.

I woke to the smell of fake mutton. So did Butter, and she started drooling. That Lab thinks she's a gourmet, but she's fooling herself. No foodie would lust over these stinky MREs. Even their name is fake. They call them Meals Ready to Eat, but they aren't.

They need hot water, time, and an undiscerning palate to be edible. I only eat them to maintain my nutrient intake, but I wish Sabrina would stop doctoring them with those bogus aromas; I just don't have the heart to tell her. She does her best to deal with this war, the heat, and the men, and she has no one to look after her but me. I try to protect her while pretending I don't care because I don't want to ruin my reputation. Here, they all think I only care about my job, and that's fine with me. I'd rather look like a manic Malinois than a softie.

The low sun's horizontal rays hit the windows, and for a moment, this drab place looks magical. The dirty wooden floors, the plywood walls, the tired soldiers putting on their boots, even the dust speckles look dipped in gold. But it's all over by the time the handlers bring our food. Two dozen men get kitted for mission, coughing their thick morning cough; the floors creak; the smell of boots covers that of cleaning oil; and the cool morning becomes another scorching day.

I crawl out of my crate to stretch as Butter devours her food. She's getting chubby, the old girl, and that's no good for her joints. In K-9 business, the lighter, the better, but, like all unwanted pups, Butter's always hungry. That's why I let her have my food. And because it keeps me slim.

Sabrina brings my bowl. Her brown eyes are still heavy with sleep, and her hands smell like coffee as she scratches my ears.

"How're you doing, Viper? I hope we stay in today."

Brown, Butter's handler, nods.

"Me too."

His uniform is crumpled and his dark face tired; but then they all are. Our humans have been struggling since the Taliban went crazy with the IEDs. In the last few weeks, the insurgents buried hundreds of improvised explosive devices around the base. That's why we patrol outside the wire every day to find them. But the danger, the dust, and the heat are getting to our soldiers, and they smell pooped. All but Silver, Guinness's handler, who's on a roll.

Oops. I forgot to mention Guinness, my other partner. She's a gorgeous German shepherd, all black but for her brown eyebrows, and she has a wicked sense of humor for a German.

Butter finishes her food and eyes mine, so I nudge my bowl toward her. She wags her tail in thanks.

"Me too. I could do with a day off for a change," she mumbles as she sniffs my food.

Guinness ups her black muzzle in an upward dog, raises her rear in a downward dog, and finishes her yoga practice with a shake. She glances at Silver, who's bringing her bulletproof vest.

"No rest for the weary today, boys and girls."

Silver buckles her in. Brown does the same with Butter as Sabrina fits mine, and we file toward the heavy green gates where the soldiers are waiting.

Butter and Brown are leading today, and Guinness and Silver bring up the rear. That leaves Sabrina and I in the middle, breathing everyone's dust. Oh well. It still beats lying in the crate counting your toes.

The metal hinges scream as the gates crack open. Butter wags her golden tail like it's a flag as she steps out, leading Brown on his thirty-foot leash. She takes a few steps, raises her nose to sniff the wind, and stays put.

I don't know if she's working on her tan or figuring out what leash to wear, but she keeps us baking under the brutal sun until I can't take it anymore.

"No rush, Butter, *chérie*. Please, take your time."

Somewhere behind me, Guinness growls.

"Shut up, Viper. Butter knows what she's doing better than you."

I can't argue with that, so I bite my tongue and dance on my feet until Butter gets moving. Today's mission is to comb the village compound, searching for explosives. It's a hot mile in the sun since the scraggly bushes scattered through the desert couldn't shade a malnourished mouse, and, other than them and the mud wall surrounding the compound, there's nothing but scorching orange desert.

My paws burn as we shuffle forward breathing the dust risen by two dozen boots. I'm not loving it, but a job is a job, and the sooner we're done, the sooner we'll be back inside the wire.

The village is nothing but a handful of mud huts surrounded by a tall wall. As usual, we divide into teams. We K-9s search inside the houses while our soldiers wait outside, their arms ready, in case we find trouble.

I'm glad to be in the shade. Bombs I can deal with, but there's only so much heat I can take. And the job's easy. I whiz through the first hut, all empty but for a rug and a jug. The narrow slits in the walls kept it cool, but the heat swallows me once I step out. I pant and wag my tail to Sabrina.

"Anything?"

"Nope."

She wipes the sweat off her face and follows me to our last hut. The other two teams will take care of the rest, and we'll head back to base in no time.

There's no door, so I push in through the curtain. This hut is just like the other — baked earth floor, a rug, and a water jug — but for a painted chest and the two men glaring at me. They smell like hate. That's nothing new — after six years of service, I have yet to meet a native who likes me — but something about them rubs me wrong.

Their baggy shalwar kameez flutter in the breeze as they stand near each other, doing nothing. They ogle me like I'm a snake, not a trained K-9 on a mission, and I wonder what they're up to.

I sniff their feet, their fists, their clothes. There's no hint of explosives, but their sweat smells like they're scheming something. I don't trust them. I bet they're planning something treacherous.

But I'm a trained explosive detecting K-9. I didn't come here to look for hate and revenge. There's no shortage of either here in

Kandahar. My mission is to find explosives, and they don't have any. Time to move on.

But I can't.

I stare at them and they glare back. Their eyes say they'd love to kill me. But they can't. What can they be up to? I don't know what to do.

"You OK, Viper?"

That's Sabrina. She's getting antsy. I need to make up my mind, but I can't. My training says that my work here is done, but my instinct tells me otherwise.

"Hey, Viper. Nice quarters you moved into."

That's Guinness. She's pissed. They all are, standing under the killer sun waiting for me to be done. But I don't know what to do. My hackles are up, my skin prickles, and something stirs in my gut. I feel something's wrong, but I don't know what. If I found any trace of explosives, I'd give the signal and the soldiers would take them away. But I have nothing but a hunch, and I'm a professional. My mission is finding explosives, not haters.

I follow my training and step out to find our soldiers waiting, their arms ready. Sabrina sighs with relief.

"Anything?"

I sort of wag my tail.

"Not really."

We file back into formation to return to camp. I can't wait to be back inside the wire, but I'm terrified that I made a mistake. I bet I missed something. What were those two up to? I'd love to go back if I could.

Somewhere behind me, Guinness barks.

"What the heck took you so long?"

I'm tired and annoyed, and I know she is too. But this isn't a conversation I'll bark across the desert, even though most soldiers don't speak dog, so they wouldn't understand us. I ignore Guinness and drag myself forward with my dust-coated tongue hanging to my knees as we crawl back. Butter takes her sweet time sniffing every speckle of dust like she didn't just do it on the way over.

Then she stops.

She raises her muzzle to sniff something by the corner of the wall. The sun beats on us, but she freezes with her golden head held high and ears pricked like she's posing. I sniff that way too, but I get nothing, and I lose it.

"Do not rush, Butter, *chérie*. We have nothing better to do than to enjoy this dust all day."

Butter cocks her head. She opens her mouth to tell me where to put it when the earth explodes, and she rolls to the ground in a cloud of dust.

2

Did I feel guilty? I had no time.

By the time our soldiers dropped to the ground and opened fire, the orange dust had cut our vision to a couple of feet. The gunfire stopped as fast as it started, and we gathered ourselves from the ground. Sabrina spat out the dust, wiped her mouth with her sleeve, and pulled me back with both hands when I sprung to check on Butter.

Just a few leaps away, my old friend lay motionless in a puddle of blood, looking dead. But Brown kneeled by her side, tightening a tourniquet around her paw, so I knew she must be alive. I pulled forward to see how she was doing, but Sabrina dragged me back.

"Not now, Viper. We don't have time. Half the men will go after the insurgents who shot Butter, and we must show them the way."

That I can do. I glance back, where Guinness leaps forward, dragging Silver. I know they'll look after Butter, so I bark my goodbye as I follow Sabrina.

"Good luck, Butter. We're going to get the ice-holes who shot you. Hang in there, my friend. I'll see you inside the wire."

I sniff the gunpowder, track the scent, sprint uphill behind some scruffy bushes, then canter downhill into a dry riverbed where the smell grows stronger. I follow it, inhaling dust with every breath until I fall upon the gun tucked in the elbow of a twisted tree.

I sit next to it. Sabrina gives the signal, and the men rush over.

"It's still hot from the shot," Emil says. "This must be it."

"Of course. But that doesn't tell us who shot it. Sabrina? Can Viper track them down?"

Sabrina lets me sniff the weapon. Not for explosives, this time, but for the scent of whoever held it close. The sharp odor of gunpowder overpowers every other smell, so I struggle. I sniff and sniff until I catch a musky odor. And mint, which counts for nothing, since here everyone drinks mint tea.

"Viper, track," Sabrina says.

No kidding.

I ramble at first, struggling to find my stride. But I soon find my groove and follow the track that takes us back to the village in a roundabout way. The scent gets stronger and stronger, and I drag Sabrina back to the hut that puzzled me this morning.

The two men are still here, reeking of hate and glaring at me, but there are half a dozen more surrounding them, all wearing shalwar kameez that hide their skinny bodies and possibly suicide vests. Their brothers, sons, and grandsons, some just toddlers, came to protect them, and they all smell like hate.

The stench of stress sweat overpowers the gunpowder on their clothes, but I didn't train all these years for nothing. I sniff every inch of every man like it's going out of style, and I sit by the elder to point him out. The soldiers handcuff him and take him away as I move to the next man, then the next.

A crooked man with eyes the color of storm wants to kick me so badly he bites his lip to stop. I know he's the one who shot Butter, and I fight the urge to open his throat right here and now. I point him out and move on to the last one. He's just a kid, not old enough to sprout a beard, but he stinks of guilt just like the others, and his clenched fists betray his hate.

I wag my tail to Sabrina.

"That's it."

"Are you sure?"

"Yep. The others don't smell like gunpowder. I bet they all knew, but nobody else touched that weapon."

We file back to the base, and I sniff every step, like Butter did, wishing I wasn't such an ass. I hope the last words Butter ever heard from me weren't a snarl. We both deserve better than that.

The green gates open, and we file inside to safety, but that's the last thing on my mind. The air is thick with grief, and I wonder if Butter's still alive.

She lies motionless in the middle of the yard, her stretcher surrounded by grief-stricken men. Brown and Silver work on wrapping her paw. Guinness hunches by her head, her ears flat with worry, smelling like sorrow.

I sit by her shoulder, and she leans on me.

"How is she?"

"Not well. They called for a helicopter. Should be here any moment."

Just heartbeats later, the growling of the engines deafens us while the blades raise a sea of dust. We're just two feet away, but I struggle to discern Butter's face as the soldiers lift the stretcher.

She doesn't move as they race to load her in. The last thing I see is her mangled paw wrapped in a white bandage; then she's gone.

"I love you, Butter. You'll be OK," Guinness barks.

I wish I could say it, but I can't. I've never said, "I love you." So I do my best:

"Take care, Butter. I can't wait to have you back. I'll save my mutton just for you."

Brown climbs in the helicopter, and they're off.

I choke with sorrow as I watch the flying monster take my friend. I know I'll never see Butter again, and it's all my fault.

3

After that, our nights became lonely and sad. Guinness and I lie in our crates with Butter's empty bed between us, reminding us of our loss. Like we needed reminding.

But, as day after day went by without news from Butter, I felt relieved. That meant she was alive. I'd seen her paw, so I knew she'd never return. But Guinness didn't, so she spends her days waiting for her. Whenever the trucks come to bring mail, supplies, or new recruits, Guinness sprints to the gate, hoping they brought Butter. But they never do, so she comes back with her head hanging low, smelling like grief. It hurts to watch her, but I don't have the heart to crush her hope.

One evening when two trucks came and left without Butter, Guinness set her nose on her paws and whined.

"Oh, how I miss her. You know, Viper, there's something about these Canadians. They're just nice. Not like us."

I cocked my head.

"I beg your pardon?"

"No offense, Viper, but nobody would call us nice. We may be loyal, reliable, and hard-working, but nice?"

"You forgot attractive and modest, *hein*?"

Guinness slapped her tail to the floor in a weak dog smile.

"Common, Viper, you're not offended, are you? Would you really compare yourself to Butter in the nice department?"

"I would not, but that's not so bad. Some folks are just too nice. You and I would never let someone walk all over us. Nor would we fall apart because some ice-hole doesn't like us. Butter might. In our line of business, that's a liability. There's always someone whose paws you must step on. They won't like you, but so what? We aren't here to be popular; we're here to do our job."

Guinness agreed, though she hates thinking that Butter isn't perfect. But she's not. She's delightful, but perfect? Nobody is.

Now that Butter's gone, Guinness and I take turns in the lead, and I discover that I hate being in the rear even more than being in the middle. I dislike the dust, of course, but even more, I dread the thought of Guinness missing an IED. How silly is that? Guinness is a well-trained professional and a K-9, and she's got her own job to do. But I got so attached to her that just the thought of seeing her hurt gives me the heebie-jeebies.

At first, I thought it was because of Butter getting shot. If Guinness gets hurt, I'll be the only K-9 left. Terrible, *quoi*? I have to keep her safe. But then she got that letter.

The mail truck came and left without Butter, as usual. Guinness returned from the gate and lay her nose on her paws when Silver brought her a brown package.

"This came in for you."

Guinness pricked her ears.

"For me?"

We K-9s seldom get mail. I, for one, never get any. No wonder since we can't read. We can smell it, of course, but the scent has already faded by the time it arrives. And who even remembers us? I've had no one since Jinx died. And he couldn't write worth a damn.

"Yep. For you. K-9 Corporal Guinness Van Jones. Should I open it for you?" Silver asked.

Guinness glared.

"Hell no. Thanks."

Silver shrugged and left. Guinness sniffed every inch of the box as if she were looking for IEDs, then dispatched it with a quick bite and shook out its insides. She checked them one by one, and her ears flattened.

Bad news? I wondered. But it was none of my business, so I turned around to clean my privates, pretending I wasn't watching.

"Viper?"

"Yep."

"I got a package from home."

"Home?"

"Upstate New York. My mom's place."

"Oh."

"She lives with Jones. He taught me how to swear."

Wow. This Jones must be a talented guy. I've never met a lady with a more colorful vocabulary.

"Good news?"

"Sort of. Mom's alive and well, and she sends her best wishes."

Guinness shows me the picture of the best-looking K-9 I've ever seen, and that's a tall order since I'm a Malinois. German shepherds are our rivals, and it's not a lighthearted competition — it goes to the core of who we are. We're more driven — they're more balanced. They're stronger — we're leaner. And they think they're smarter, but they're wrong. But Guinness's mom would turn the head of any male who walks on four paws and fans himself with a tail.

"She's beautiful."

"That's just the beginning. Mom is wise, patient, and funny. I wish I grew up to be like her, but I took after my father."

"He couldn't be that bad."

I cock my head and take in Guinness's elegant muzzle, her fluffy tail, and those golden eyebrows that get my heart pumping. I'd never been into eyebrows before I met Guinness.

"Thanks, Viper. You care for some popcorn?"

"Don't mind if I do."

I love popcorn. It's nothing but air with a touch of butter flavor, but it makes you feel full, and that's good. I've gained a few pounds since Butter left, and there's no one to save my food for.

"Anything else?"

Guinness looks puzzled. She cocks her head to stare at a picture, then scratches her right ear with her hind paw to help herself think.

"I guess so."

"What's up?"

"There."

She points to the picture of a dog like I've never seen before. He's orange, but he'd look just like Guinness if he wasn't the wrong color.

"Who's that?"

"Beats me."

She grabs the letter and goes to find Silver. I'm half asleep by the time she returns with the answer.

"He seems to be my brother Fuzzy. Apparently, Mom had another litter, and they turned out orange."

"Orange shepherds? How can that be?"

Guinness glares at me.

"What do you think, Viper? Their father was a free dog, a golden retriever named Ranger. That's why the kids turned out weird."

"Oh."

I don't know if this is good news or bad news. Guinness's mom going interbreed may open Guinness's mind, but she doesn't look excited about her new brother.

"Jones says the kid takes after me and went into the military. Keep an eye on the new recruits, he says, just in case he ends up there."

I look for something to say, and nothing intelligent comes to mind. But I'm not the sort of guy who'd let that detail stop me.

"Well. With that color, he'll be hard to tell from the dust, so the Taliban are less likely to shoot him."

Guinness's eyebrows join as she frowns at me.

I flatten my ears and close my eyes, pretending I'm asleep. What a freaking charmer!

4

Fortunately, thanks to the Taliban, I didn't have much time to make a fool of myself. Guinness and I spent our days searching for IEDs, weapons, and suspects. We rarely had time for ourselves other than the evenings when we chatted in our side of the hangar while the humans played cards with the most wanted men on the other side.

"I'll raise you Chemical Ali against the Anthrax Lady," Ben said.

Fred shook his head in disbelief.

"Seriously? How about some swamp land somewhere?"

The others laughed, but they weren't kidding. To help them recognize the wanted men, the army had issued playing cards with their pictures. Instead of kings and queens, our soldiers played poker with angry mustached men.

Guinness watched them deep in thought.

"Do you think that works?" she asked.

"Dunno. To me, they all look alike. I couldn't tell them apart but for the smell."

That reminded me of the day Butter got shot. I never had the guts to tell Guinness, but I know that the men who shot Butter are the same two I let go. I'd bet my tail against an empty bowl of kibble that I'm right. I recognized their rancid stench of revenge and the fire in their hooded eyes.

The memory of that day weighs on me. I think of it every night and every day and tell myself that it's my fault that Butter got shot. Butter would be here today if I wasn't such a stickler for the rules and had listened to my instinct. But I let them go just because they didn't smell like explosives, like you need explosives to destroy someone. Butter's gone, and we don't even know if she's alive. And it's all my fault.

I'd love to tell Guinness and lift this weight off my soul, but I don't dare. What will she say? What if she holds me responsible and hates me forever?

Guinness pricks her ears.

"I just had an idea! They should make something like smelling cards for us. That way, we'd learn them, and we'd recognize them for sure."

"And what would we do?"

"Bring them to justice, of course. What else?"

"But that's not what we do. We are explosive-detecting K-9s. We're here to detect explosives, not to play the Avengers."

"Says who?"

She glares at me, and I shrink.

"Guinness, we are both K-9 officers, and we must play by the rules. You know that as well as I do."

Her hackles raise.

"I know no such thing. I know right from wrong, and I don't give a hoot about the rules. I have a nose to follow and a heart to listen to. And so do you."

I'm so anxious I get all prickly, and I start scratching. How do I know what's right and what's wrong? Would it be correct to detain people before they did anything? Or would that be wrong? Darned if I know.

"Guinness, you know we must obey the rules."

I wag my tail to mollify her, but it's not working.

"Seriously? You know as well as I do that the humans who make the rules don't have the commonsense Dog gave a squirrel crossing the road. And you want to abide by them? Come on, Viper!"

I shrivel. Thank Dog, she doesn't know. But she sniffs my guilt like it's painted on my forehead. She cocks her head and stares at me, then comes over to smell my butt and find out more, so I curl my tail between my legs to cover it.

"Viper, what did you do?"

"Nothing."

She yawns.

"So, what did you not do?"

This girl is too smart for her own good. And for mine. But there's no point in lying; she'll know it. I may as well come clean.

"I'm afraid I let Butter's attackers go."

Guinness doesn't raise her hackles. She doesn't even growl.

"Tell me about it."

I tell her how I found those men and how I agonized about what to do. Then I let them go, and Butter got shot. Guinness listens, her amber eyes so calm it's scary.

"You think it was them?"

"I do."

"Why?"

"They smelled like hate and revenge, just like those we picked up that smelled like gunpowder."

"Everyone here smells like hate and revenge. Even us."

I breathe.

"So, you think I was OK to let them go?"

She looks at me with pity.

"Of course not. You should have brought them over and had the humans check them. If you had, Butter might be here now."

I'm befuddled. Why isn't she mad, then?

"So, I did the wrong thing."

"Of course. But you did the Viper thing. You always play by the rules. You don't know how to do anything else. It's not your fault — you do you. But it's high time you grew up."

She turns away to lay her nose on her paws and closes her eyes, and I feel more chastised than I've ever been. And I get angry. Very angry. Who does she think she is to tell me what to do? I'm twice her age, and I have more experience than she'll ever have. My whole life, I've done my job the best I could and played by the rules. And this green K-9 thinks she knows better? I'm so furious I fathom tasting her blood, and she smells it.

"Go ahead if you think you'll feel better," she says, without opening her eyes.

My rage melts, and guilt takes over. I crawl into my crate to lay my nose on my paws. In my mind, I see Butter's sad eyes.

"There's more to one's life than a job, Viper," she says.

I wish I had a hole to crawl in.

5

My anger against Guinness didn't last long. She just raised her eyebrows and wagged her fluffy tail, and I got hooked again.

It took me a while to understand that my feelings for her went beyond friendship. I couldn't believe that an old dog — I'm seven and a half, that's like more than 50 human years — could fall for a female less than half his age. But my heart flips when I hear her bark, and my insides turn squishy every time she sniffs my butt, so even an old curmudgeon like me has to admit that I've found The One.

So I started courting her the best I knew how: I left her the best place by the fan, I saved Sabrina's special treats just for her, and I did my best to not be an ice-hole, but she didn't even notice. And that's OK. Being ignored is no fun, but being laughed at? That's worse.

I didn't lose hope. I offered her my butt to sniff every morning — there isn't much to learn since we're together all the time — but that's how dogs communicate. Sniffing each other tells us what the other had for dinner, the mood they're in, and if they feel like dating.

That's how I knew that Guinness had the runs last week after she snitched a bar of Dove soap from the showers. She's a big fan, and she finished it in one sitting, as witnessed by her bubbly pink, sweet-smelling diarrhea. I didn't mention it, of course, but I filed that info in case I happen upon a bar of Dove. Wouldn't that make a lovely gift? We dogs have no money, so we can't buy flowers, wine, or chocolate. That makes it hard to woo someone — other than letting them smell you.

But Guinness didn't notice, even though she sniffs my butt every day. Isn't that odd? Even Sabrina noticed, and she never smells me. But she's a girly girl, Sabrina, all into lipstick and fake eyelashes, even though she doesn't need them. Any human at the camp would love to date her, but she's not interested.

"Then why tart yourself up?" I asked.

She shrugged.

"Just to remember that I'm still a girl."

That made no sense. How could you forget? Even if I did, I'd remember every time I clean my privates. Maybe humans don't clean their privates? Weird creatures. Either way, Sabrina knows I've got my eye on Guinness, and she's worried.

"Viper, are you sure this isn't your midlife crisis?"

"What's that?"

"It's when mature men mourn losing their youth, so they drive fast cars and date young girls."

"Sabrina, I don't drive. And, no offense, but I never met a girl I wanted to date. Even the pretty ones lack in the tail department."

Sabrina laughed and brushed me until I got all shiny, then got me a new collar. She always compliments me when Guinness is around, but Guinness doesn't seem to notice. So, to get her attention, I started bragging.

"If they left those prisoners with me, I'd get the truth out of them in no time."

"Really? I didn't think we were allowed to interrogate prisoners. Have you done it before?"

I cock my head.

"Sure. Haven't you?"

"No. How did you get them to cooperate?"

"I barked."

"Really? That's all it took?"

"It depends. But for me, that's all it took."

I watch her file that, and I wonder what she's thinking. That's the thing with Guinness. You never know what she's got in mind until she comes out of left field with some weird idea.

"Have you ever killed anyone?"

As I said.

"I thought we were talking interrogation. Why do you ask?"

She looks away, and I know she's about to lie. That's the thing about dogs. Unlike people, we don't lie staring into each other's faces. We couldn't get away with it anyhow because lies stink.

"Just curious."

I wonder who she plans to kill. I hope it's not me.

I run our roster, but I can't come up with anyone she hates, so I tell her.

"Go for the throat. All this stuff humans teach you in apprehension, like grab onto the arm and such? That's for when you have plenty of time and good backup. But when it gets real, go for the throat."

Guinness's eyes glaze over in thought, and I'd love to sniff her butt and find out what she's thinking, but that's against the protocol.

I try to think about something to say, but nothing comes to mind. Except...

"Would you like some popcorn?"

Guinness cocks her head. Popcorn is her weakness. That, and bacon. But I couldn't get bacon in Kandahar if I sold my tail. The Afghans are Muslims, so they don't eat pork. They think pigs are dirty and useless. That alone explains why I could never be a Muslim. But Sabrina had gotten me some popcorn, and I hid it, waiting for the perfect time. Popcorn for dogs is like champagne for humans: it sets the mood.

Guinness wags her tail.

"I'd love it."

I pull the popcorn bag from under my bed and spread it on the floor. Guinness and I pick one kernel after another, staring into each other's eyes, and I've never felt closer to her. She raises her eyebrows, and my insides turn hot and squishy. We're finally getting somewhere.

I crawl and lick her nose. She wiggles her eyebrows, and I'm ready to jump out of my skin when I hear boots.

It's Silver. Her eyes bright with tears, she kneels to hug Guinness.

"What happened?"

"Butter. She made it."

Like seriously? You interrupted us for that? I knew that a month ago!

"But they had to cut off her leg. She'll never come back."

6

Guinness wilted like a snowman in the sun. Her ears flattened, her head drooped, and her sexy, confident scent turned into the stench of dejection. Her sad puppy eyes tore at my heart.

"What are we going to do, Viper?"

Oh, how young she is! Our Guinness is so wise and confident that I forgot she's only three. She hasn't lived through years of this war that sucks you dry and steals your youth, your friends, and your hope, leaving you hollow inside. You learn to expect nothing but misery and rejoice if you get something better.

I sighed and licked her nose.

"We'll do what we always do, Guinness. We'll do our job. We'll patrol, we'll look for IEDs, we'll have each other's back, and we'll protect our humans, so they don't end up like Butter."

Her grief chokes me. I wish I could help, but Guinness wants Butter, and I can't bring her back. Nor do I want to. The old girl deserves better. I hope she has found peace and comfort wherever she is and gets real mutton every day. I hope she doesn't miss us one bit, no matter how much we miss her.

"I'm sorry, Guinness. I wish I could help."

She lays her nose on her paws and closes her eyes, and the scent of her anguish reminds me of losing Jinx.

Jinx was my twin. Not my littermate — we had seven of those — but looking at Jinx was like seeing myself in a mirror. We were inseparable, and no one could tell us apart.

When we got imported from Belgium, we were assigned different handlers, so we lived in separate homes. But we still trained together every day, we could read each other's thoughts, and we loved playing tricks on our handlers.

My human was Andrew. He had two kids and a large wife he called Mom. She lived to clean. She went nuts chasing every hair I shed and went berserk every time Andrew and I came home covered in mud. She drove me crazy, but at least I had Jinx to vent to.

"She vacuums the house and then weighs the hair. Who'd do that? And why? I don't know where Andrew found her, but I sure hope he takes her back."

Jinx spat the ball we were chasing.

"I don't know, brother. But at least you don't have a cat."

"A cat? Are you crazy? Where did you get a cat?"

Jinx flattened his ears and looked away, so I knew he'd brought that upon himself.

"I found him in the gutter. He must have washed in with the rain. It's just a little tabby, but he's a pain in the butt. He follows me everywhere and sniffs my stuff when I go to the bathroom. Imagine that! A cat! And he's deaf. He doesn't wake up when I bark."

"Why on earth did you pick him up, *hein*?"

"I don't know! He was all soaked and muddy, crying and smelling dejected. I couldn't leave him there to drown. I picked him by the scruff of his neck, shook him to get rid of the mud, and brought him home. The kids love him, but he likes me more, so he follows me like a shadow. He's only as big as an onion, and he stinks even worse, but I don't have the heart to tell him no. He wouldn't hear anyhow; he's just a cat and deaf too, for Dog's sake. But he's the bane of my existence."

I stare at Jinx, and he looks away, so I know he's lying. He loves that cat, but he's ashamed to admit it. I would be, too, if I loved a cat.

Life went on. I dealt with Mom, and he dealt with his cat until the day we decided to play a switch on our trainers. I went to his home, and he went to mine. We knew the humans wouldn't notice if we played it right.

I briefed Jinx.

"Shake before you step in the house, and ignore the vacuum cleaner. It's on all the time. Avoid the female and ignore the kids unless they feed you treats. Don't let her catch you on the sofa, or she'll have a conniption."

"That doesn't sound like much fun."

"Who said anything about fun? We're doing it for the experience, to see how good we've got it and feel better about our plot in life. So, what are my instructions?"

"The potty place is by the tall hedge. Don't drink from the toilets; the water smells like chlorine. And be nice to Turbo."

"Turbo?"

"The cat. He purrs like a broken engine, so we call him Turbo. He's my... my friend."

"I thought you hated him."

Jinks looks away.

"That was long ago. Now he's my friend. So, be nice to Turbo. Everything else is fair game."

I went home with Jinx's trainer, and he went home with mine.

Tricking the humans into thinking you're their dog was a piece of cake. Fun too! Jinx's car was littered with kids' toys, fast food wrappers, and all sorts of bits and bobs, not clean like ours. It was awesome! I had to refrain from checking everything out, and I reminded myself to not go sniffing around Jinx's house like I was new there.

I did well until I stepped through the door and heard this terrible siren noise. Then this tabby cat attacked me and tried to claw my eyes out. It took all my self-control to not tear him to pieces. I told him:

"Relax, Turbo. I'm Viper, Jinx's twin. We switched places for the night. He'll be back tomorrow."

Turbo didn't listen. He hissed, spat, and tried to kill me. The audacity! It was easy to dispatch him, but I knew Jinx would get mad, so I endured Turbo's foolish antics, hissing and roaring like a fire engine until Jinx's trainer grabbed him by the scruff of his neck and locked him up.

"You had to get that useless cat from the gutter, and now he's lost his mind."

He cleaned my scratches with plenty of hydrogen peroxide and very little patience. Boy, was I glad to switch back the next day.

"Your Turbo is out of his mind. I had a hard time keeping my eyes safe."

Jinx glared at me.

"If you touched one hair of his back..."

"Then what?"

He sighed and got himself together.

"Sorry, Viper, I just love that kitten. Other than you, he's my best friend."

He sure did. He loved him enough to die for him, not much later.

7

The day Butter got shot had been atrocious for us all, but finding out that she lost her leg and won't return destroyed the camp morale. Guinness was dejected. So was I, and so were the humans, even those who didn't work with her, since Butter's friendly tail wag never failed to bring a smile to people's faces.

Guinness and I couldn't replace her even if we tried. There's something special about Labradors; like puppies, they touch a soft spot in people's hearts, and everyone loves them. Guinness and I are loyal and reliable, and we work hard to keep everyone safe. But nobody ever comes to pet us or bring us treats other than our handlers. And that's fine with me since I'm not into PDA. And neither is Guinness.

That's why, when Silver came to hug her, Guinness shrank. She wanted to bolt, but she didn't since she didn't want to hurt Silver's feelings.

"What happened?"

"I have fantastic news! We're going home!"

"Home?"

"Yes. We're going back home, you and I! We'll take long hikes in the forest without looking for IEDs, we'll play in the snow, we'll eat bacon and watch TV! What do you think of that?"

Guinness cocked her head.

"Really?"

"Yes. We were due to go back a while ago, but we lost Butter and Brown, and we were short one team. But they have a new K-9 unit coming, so they'll let us go."

"When?"

"Soon."

Guinness jumped up to lick Silver's face, licked my nose, then started chasing her tail like a silly pup. She caught it and fell into a panting heap, smiling from one black ear to the other.

I wagged my tail to show her I was happy for her, but I was devastated. What will I do without her? How can I be without her? And I'm not even talking work, though it's terrible to have no partner.

"I'm so happy for you, Guinness. I know you can't wait to be home."

She sniffed my sadness, so she came to lick my nose.

"Thanks, Viper. I'll miss you."

"I'll miss you even more."

In her heart, she's already gone. She can't wait to be home, away from this miserable war. I can't blame her, but boy, how I'll miss her. I try to not be a party pooper.

"What's the first thing you'll do when you go back?"

"I'll find the biggest pile of snow, and I'll roll in it, eat it, and bury myself in it. Then I'll come out and start over."

"What if it isn't winter?"

That's another thing about being here. Every day is just like the others: hot and dusty. Since I don't have a calendar, I don't even know if it's summer or winter. And it doesn't matter, since here they're just the same. I miss watching the seasons change. I love winter's snow, spring's mud, summer's swims, and chasing leaves in the fall.

Guinness wags her tail.

"If there's no snow, I'll roll in the mud. That's even better."

Every morning and every night, she asks Silver if it's time, and every time she breaks my heart again. She can't wait to be gone, and she doesn't even know she's hurting me.

Sabrina does.

"I'm so sorry, Viper. I know you'll miss her, but remember we're getting a new team. You'll make a new friend."

See, that's the thing about humans. Even the smart ones can't put themselves in your paws. Just because this new K-9, whoever it is, has four legs and a tail doesn't mean we'll be friends. We may even hate each other. That happens to humans too — you'd think she'd understand.

But it is what it is. I'd better make the most of every moment left with Guinness. I'll have plenty of time to be sad when she's gone. So, Sabrina and I decide to have a party, and she's in charge of the details.

"We'll make two cakes: One for Silver, one for Guinness. Silver's will be sweet. I saved my MRE deserts to build it. But I don't know what to do for Guinness. What would she like?"

"Bacon."

"Wouldn't we all? But I can't get bacon. What else?"

"A cheeseburger? With a nice candle?"

"Let me see what I can do."

When the last day came, Guinness was so excited that Silver had to chase her all over the hangar to buckle on her bulletproof vest.

"This is our last day! Our last patrol! We're going home tomorrow!"

"I know. But we still have this last job, and we must do it well. Be careful, OK?"

"Of course," Guinness barked, running around the hangar to chase the zoomies. It was her turn to lead that day, but she was so wild I worried she'd get distracted.

"Hey, Guinness? How about you take the rear and let me lead today?"

You'd think she'd be grateful, but no! She growled at me.

"Are you out of your mind? Just because you're male, you think you can lead better? I've done this a hundred times. I can do it just as well as you can. Even better."

I flattened my ears and went to look for Sabrina. These darn feminists! Can't appreciate a chivalrous gesture!

Sabrina buckled me in.

"We're all set for the party. Emil donated a meatloaf MRE, and Ben gave us two tortillas to make Guinness's cake. It's not exactly a burger, but it will have to do."

"And we'll light a match for a candle."

"Good thought."

She clipped her leash to my collar, and we filed to the gate for Guinness's last patrol.

8

The green gates creak open, and Guinness dances out like she's late for a party, dragging Silver behind on her thirty-foot-long leash. The soldiers file behind them, and Sabrina and I close the rear. It's just another hot and dusty day outside the wire, but the deep silence of the desert unsettles me. The memory of Butter getting shot hits me like a ton of bricks, and I wish Guinness would let me lead the patrol, but there's no point in asking again; she's stubborn as a mule. So, I bark.

"Guinness?"

"Yes."

"Be careful."

She glances at me like I've lost it, then pushes forward without answering. But what is there to say? "Thanks for telling me, Viper; without you, I was going to be careless as usual."

Guinness sniffs her way step by step, and nothing happens. We cross the open field without even a mouse bothering us, and we reach the compound. Everything's still and quiet, just as it should be.

I start thinking I'm just paranoid because Guinness is leaving tomorrow. One after the other, the soldiers round the corner and file along the eight-foot-tall wall, and I follow. It's all good until something flies over and lands between Guinness and Silver.

It looks like a baseball, but I've never seen them play baseball here. The thing rolls slowly toward Silver, then stops a few feet from her boots. She stares at it, then drops the leash and screams:

"Run, Guinness. Run."

That makes no sense. What is she saying? Guinness doesn't get it either, and she turns her head to stare at Silver.

"Run? Run where?"

Guinness screens the desert, looking for a perpetrator, but nothing moves as far as the eye can see. Silver drops to the ground, and Guinness rushes to help her just as the earth shudders under our feet.

The ball bursts in flames, and a wall of noise crashes into me as the explosion blasts Guinness high in the air. She twists and twirls before crashing in a motionless heap as I bite the dust.

Our fire is fast and furious, but our soldiers can't see anything beyond the orange dust that drowns us. The shooting stops, and we run to help Guinness and Silver, who were nearest the blast.

I can tell Silver's dead as soon as I get near her. It's not just the pool of blood or her unblinking eyes. It's that funny smell dead people get when life flies out of them. We all learned it after so much war. All but Guinness.

She lays her paws on Silver's chest and licks her face.

"Come on, Silver, get up. We're leaving tomorrow, remember?"

Silver's frozen eyes stare at the sky. She doesn't answer.

Guinness grabs her vest to pull her up.

"Come on, Silver. We have no time. Let's finish this patrol and go home!"

The soldiers try to pull her away, but she'll have none of it.

"Let me be! Help Silver! She needs to get up! We're leaving tomorrow!"

"She can't get up, Guinness."

She looks at me like I'm crazy.

"Sure, she can. She has to. Don't you remember? We're leaving tomorrow!"

The men lift Silver on a stretcher. Guinness dashes to the head of the file to lead us back inside the wire, but they won't let her, so she follows Silver's stretcher as I lead us back.

As soon as the green gates close behind us, Guinness starts barking.

"Come on, people! Do something! We're back inside now; we're safe! Put on a tourniquet! Call the helicopter. Do something! Remember, like you did with Butter?"

The soldiers stand frozen, watching her with teary eyes. Guinness runs from one to the other, nudges them and barks. No one moves.

She thinks they don't understand, so she pulls out Silver's first-aid kit from her equipment and drops it on her chest.

"There. Her first-aid kit. Come on, everyone! What's wrong with you? Start an IV! Give her something! Call the helicopter! She needs help!"

A soldier tries to pet her, but she leaps aside. Another one wants to pull her away, but Guinness bares her teeth and growls. She's about to sink them in his flesh when Sabrina takes out her first-aid kit.

Guinness relents.

"Finally! I thought nobody was going to do anything. What took you all so long?"

Sabrina fills her syringe. The long needle gleams as it catches the sun.

"Sorry, Guinness."

The needle sinks deep into Guinness's neck, and she falls to the ground

9

What? My jaw falls. I turn to Sabrina, bare my teeth, and growl.

"What the heck did you do that for?"

Sabrina drops the syringe to check Guinness's pulse.

"Sorry, Viper. I had to calm her down before she hurt someone. You saw she was out of control, and you know what happens when K-9s attack people."

That I do.

After graduating from our training, Jinx and I started work. Andrew and I got deployed to Iraq, but Jinx and his handler landed a cushy stateside job, watching paint dry someplace or other. I got news from him through the grapevine every now and then, and I knew he was well.

I was envious. Jinx stayed home to enjoy good food, take mud baths, and watch the leaves turn while I listened to the call to prayer five times a day. What strings did he pull? How did he get to stay home while I breathed dust and ate MREs?

When I stopped hearing about him, I didn't worry. Jinx was more likely to get hit by a car than step on a mine wherever he was. I just hoped he'd get fat from living the good life, so I could laugh at him when we met.

Then Andrew and I went home. It was nice to walk without searching for IEDs, soak in the rain, and take mud baths. But Mom drove me nuts. She wiped my feet every time I came in and had me wear booties when it rained. A Belgian Malinois with red booties! Humiliating!

Andrew didn't like it much either, so one morning he went to buy cigarettes and didn't return. A few days later, the army assigned me a new handler.

George checked my papers.

"You had a brother Jinx?"

My heart froze.

"Jinx is my twin."

He looked into my eyes and I smelled pity.

"Sorry, Viper. Jinx died."

"Jinx died? How?"

"He got injured, and the vet had to put him to sleep."

"Injured? How did he get injured? On the job?"

"Yes, but not the way you'd think. It says here that Jinx's handler shot him."

My throat tightens, and my hackles rise. That's got to be a lie. I know this man. I know his home, his family, even his cat. How could he shoot Jinx? And why?

"Why?"

"Jinx attacked him, and the man had to shoot him to stay alive."

That day was the worst of my life, but today came close. Silver died, Guinness went berserk, and the insurgents got away with it. I hope I never see a day like this again.

The soldiers covered Silver with the American flag and stood guard around her, their faces contorted with grief. They all knew they could be under that flag. Unlike missing an IED, which could be someone's mistake, that grenade was nobody's fault. Just Silver's bad luck.

The helicopter lands to take Silver and Guinness. Silver won't be back. But Guinness?

She lies on her side smelling like no other dog I ever sniffed. I wonder what she's dreaming about. Is she running in the fields, chasing squirrels? Eating bacon? Rolling in the snow? I hope she gets to do all that again, even if that means she won't return. Grief chokes me as I lick her nose one last time.

Sabrina pats her shoulder.

"What a great K-9."

"You think she'll ever come back?"

Sabrina shrugs.

"I don't know. She's in shock, but she may recover. Some do, some don't. You want her back?"

I don't know. I'd love to see her again, but I know she hates it here. This war stole everyone dear to her: First Butter, then Silver. I don't think she'd be happy here.

The engines growl, and the helicopter lifts off in a cloud of orange dust, taking her away. I watch the monster grow smaller and smaller as the noise dies down, and I wish I told Guinness how I loved her instead of listening to my pride. What an awful waste!

"Until we meet again, my love."

10

Since Sabrina and I are the only K-9 unit left, we're so busy with patrol, training, and searches that we never have a dull moment from dusk to dawn.

But at night I lie in my crate with nothing to do but listen to the men snore. Once in a while, someone screams, and I wonder what horrors they dream about. I hope they wake up soon to escape their fears. I wish I did too, but my demons won't quit because they're real. I remember Guinness, Butter, and Silver and what this darn war did to them and to the rest of us. And I'm wary.

War is my job. It's what I'm trained to do, so it's what I do, whether I like it or not. Being a K-9 is my career, and it gives my life meaning. But, as the war took my friends one by one, I grew leery.

Sabrina struggles too. Silver was her friend, and seeing her die crushed her soul. Then the extra work, the loneliness, and the stress got to her. She doesn't eat, and she barely sleeps, so she withered like the desert bushes. I'd love to help her, but I don't know how. She needs rest, but with us two doing the work of three K-9 units, she's got no hope of getting it.

That's why I was mighty pleased when the new K-9s arrived.

It took them so long that I started thinking they were slackers. They were supposed to arrive weeks ago, but we heard nothing and I started losing hope. But one afternoon when the truck arrived I sniffed a dog.

"Hey, Sabrina! They're here! The new K-9s arrived."

"Really?"

She ran her fingers through her hair and smoothed her uniform. I could tell she wanted to take a shower and maybe even brush me to impress them, but I didn't give a hoot about what they thought. They'd taken their sweet time to arrive, and I was pissed.

"Come on. Who cares what they think? I only care about what they do! Let's go meet them."

I dashed to the truck, and she followed. A tall long-chinned man climbed out, then an orange dog that looked familiar.

The man shook Sabrina's hand and flashed a white smile.

"I'm Dick."

Sabrina's brown eyes softened as she studied him. She forgot to take back her hand.

"I'm Sabrina. We're glad to have you aboard."

"Good to be here. I think."

Dick's clear blue eyes took in the dusty trucks, the razor-wire topping the wall and the ramshackle buildings and his mouth thinned to a line. I could tell he was disappointed without even sniffing his butt.

Sabrina unglued her eyes from his to glance at the dog who dashed to bless a scraggly bush.

"And who's he?"

"That's my dog, Fury."

That settled it. I knew right then that Dick was going to be trouble. I didn't like how he looked at Sabrina; I didn't like how he held himself. And calling his partner, a trained K-9 officer, a dog? What sort of jerk would do that?

But there's something about Fury that bothers me even more. Looking at him makes my skin prickle, like when you get brushed the wrong way. I can't put my paw on it, but something about him feels weird.

Oh well. I may as well find out. I approach Fury, and he turns around politely to offer his butt. I sniff every inch of him, performing a complete evaluation. He had chicken and rice kibble for breakfast, but it's been a while. He's thirsty, and a bit stressed after his long travels, but he smells like a decent guy, even though he's just a pup. But something about him still irks me.

I turn around, and Fury sniffs my butt respectfully, wagging his fluffy tail. When he's done, we sniff each other's noses. I want to be friendly, but I notice Sabrina staring at Dick like he hung the moon, and that pisses me off. So I blurt:

"You sure took your sweet time coming over."

Fury cocks his head in surprise, and the wind fluffs his ears. How on earth can he hear with those orange things hanging like pancakes?

"I beg your pardon?"

"You were supposed to be here weeks ago. Where were you? What did you do? Did you walk all the way here?"

Fury shakes his head so hard that his ears slap his muzzle.

"And a good day to you too."

He leaves me standing there and follows Dick.

11

After Guinness left, I didn't think I could get any lonelier, but it turns out I was wrong. When Fury arrived, I learned that being lonely is not the same as being alone.

He hasn't come near me since that first day when I was rude to him. I know why, but I can't bring myself to apologize. He's just a pup, and he's new. He should be asking for my friendship. There's so much I could teach him. He may be trained to sniff explosives, but he knows nothing about camp life, about the desert, about the enemy, and even about life. It would do him good to be humble and make an overture. But he doesn't.

Night after night, we lie in our crates, pretending we don't know the other one's there, though we can smell each other's thoughts. I know Fury misses his family and wishes he wasn't here. He knows I often feel the same. But nobody says anything, so it's lonelier than being alone.

He's good at his job, I'll give him that. Whenever he leads, I watch him like a hawk, and he makes no mistakes. I can't say the same about Dick, who's so full of himself you'd think he's the bomb sniffer. Even worse, he's got Sabrina wrapped around his little finger. She's so enchanted with him that she rarely has time for me.

Even now. Sabrina's fixing my breakfast, but her cheeks are all flushed, and her eyes are full of light as she smiles at him. That hurts. I know, deep in my bones, that he's no good for her, and I wish I could tell her, but she can't see anything beyond Dick's blue eyes.

I'm crawling out of my crate to get my breakfast when the earth shudders. My ears ring from the blast as I drop to the ground, choking in a cloud of dust. The soldiers grab their weapons and start shooting blindly, so I take cover, waiting for the chaos to settle.

When it finally does, we discover that a truck loaded with explosives crashed into the green gate, warping the solid green metal into a smoking mess. Its twisted remnants hang loosely between the damaged walls.

Our impregnable camp is invulnerable no more, so there's no more safety inside the wire. That's earth-shattering.

I glance at Fury. He lays in his crate with his nose on his paws like nothing happened. He acts cool, but I can smell his anguish, and I bet he smells mine.

Poor pup. I look for something comforting to say, but I don't get to find it since Sabrina brings my bulletproof vest.

"Let's go, Viper. It's our turn to lead."

"Are you serious? We're going out on patrol after this?"

"We have to. We can't sit here waiting for the enemy to attack now that we're vulnerable. We have to go on the offensive."

We file at whatever's left of the gate as the soldiers struggle to open it. When they finally do, my heart skips a beat. The orange desert is littered with smoldering debris, for as far as I can see. Shredded tires, twisted scraps of blackened metal, bloody rags that used to be clothes, unrecognizable bits and bobs. They're all smoking, and every single one may hide an unexploded IED.

I've never had a job like this. I'll be darned if I know what I'm looking for in this field of charred remains. I glance at Sabrina.

"What are we looking for?"

She shrugs.

"The enemy, I guess."

I walk warily, sniffing the acrid fumes as my nose burns with the smell of explosives. I feel Sabrina's heart racing at the other end of the leash, and I know she's as worried as I am. It's impossible to find something here. It's like looking for a needle, not in a haystack but in a pile of needles, since everything smells like explosives.

I trudge through the debris to the open desert beyond where the fumes fade, and my smell starts to return. I take my time heading toward the village since there's no point getting there nose-blind.

I catch a whiff of human to my right. I follow my nose and the scent gets stronger, so I know I'm up to something. There we go! I leap forward, dragging Sabrina when someone behind me barks.

"Get down, Viper!"

My mind tells me that I don't take orders from dogs, but my feet are wiser, so I roll to the ground as a shot raises the dust where I was just a second ago. Another bullet grazes my vest as our men open fire.

It's hell on earth. A hail of bullets whistles over my head as I melt into the dust. I lie there, thinking it's no fun to be me when the fire stops as fast as it started. I jump up and leap forward to the shelter beyond a tiny hill where we find the insurgents. One's dead and one's wounded, and they're both just kids. I almost feel sorry for them, but I remember Butter, Silver, and Guinness, and I get over it.

That evening I lie in my crate pretending to sleep, keenly aware of Fury in the crate next to mine. I should thank him for saving my life, but I can't make myself do it.

"Hey, Viper?"

"Yes."

"I'm glad you're not dead."

"Me too, brother. Thank you."

12

Befriending Fury was like lapping cold water after patrolling the desert. After weeks of loneliness, I finally had someone who understood, since he walked in my paws.

When I was just a pup, I used to think of myself as a loner whose whole life was his job. Sure, I cared about my humans, but they changed so often they weren't worth the emotional investment.

I had to grow old to understand that my pack is my life. That's why, when Butter got shot, I lost part of my soul. Butter and I worked together for three deployments, and she knows me better than anyone else. Sometimes I wonder if she knows me better than I know myself, and that's scary.

Then Silver got killed and Guinness had her breakdown, and it got even worse. I felt lonely and hollow. I got wondering if the war was the right place for me. Was I in the wrong place, doing the wrong thing? Was my life's work worthless? Sure, I found some bombs, and I saved a few lives. But did I make the world a better place? And if I didn't, what did I do with my life?

That got me into some dark places, and I started losing it. My mentals were going downhill fast.

But then Fury came. Having him here is like fresh air to my nose and soft mud to my paws. Buddies are good for the soul.

Day after hot stinking day, we patrol this hateful land, looking for IEDs, chasing the enemy, and hoping to make it back inside the wire. But the evenings are ours to lick our charred paws and tell each other stories as the humans chat and play cards at the other end of the hangar.

I glance over to check on Sabrina, but she's missing. So is Dick. Where is she? I'm about to go looking for her when Fury asks:

"Tell me about your first mission, Viper. When was it?"

"Oh, boy. That's so long ago, I can barely remember. Let me see, *hein*? Jinx and I were twelve months old when they brought us from Belgium. We trained for months before I got deployed, six years ago, in Iraq. My first handler, Andrew, was a good man, but his female was awful. She rode him like a rented mule, so going to Iraq was like going on vacation. The army had fewer rules than his home."

"How was Iraq?"

"It was a blast. Everything was new: the heat, the smells, the food, the people. Those humans weren't used to K-9s. Everyone — the kids, the women, the elderly — stood in the sun for hours to watch us work. They had never seen dogs at work, and they couldn't believe it. There, if a dog touches a dish, they scrub it with sand and set it in the sun for 40 days to purify it before they can use it again. If they touch a dog after washing for prayer, they must scrub themselves all over again. They think that dogs are useless, filthy, and disgusting, so imagine their shock when we found a whole pod of artillery rounds and grenades under a house in Ramadi. They couldn't believe it. Andrew and I saved hundreds of lives on that mission alone.

Fury wags his tail in appreciation.

"What a great mission! What else did you do?"

"We accompanied military convoys. We always rode in the first vehicle, then popped out to check the bridges, the crossings, or anything that looked fishy. We got to stretch our legs without sniffing everyone's dust. And speak about appreciation!"

"And then?"

"When our deployment was over, we went back home. That stank since we'd gotten used to living without Mom's rules. So, one day, Andrew left, and I never heard from him again. I hope he's somewhere by the ocean, loving life."

Fury cocks his head.

"But...how about his wife? And the kids? And you?"

I sort of wag my tail. The kid's right.

"I see your point. But I can see Andrew's too. He was like a kid who loved life, and that woman sucked the joy out of him like a vacuum cleaner. That's one reason I'm wary of relationships. Not like I got many offers, but still."

"Then what?"

"The army assigned me to George, and we deployed to Afghanistan. That's when I met Butter."

"Who's Butter?"

"Butter is the nicest bomb sniffer you'll ever meet. She's Canadian since she's a yellow Lab. We worked as a team until the day she got shot. She's my best friend other than Guinness."

"Guinness?"

"Yep. Guinness is a K-9 too, but she's a German shepherd. She's an MPC, a Multi-Purpose Canine, and a darned good-looking dog.

Fury cocks his head.

"Sleek, shiny, almost black? Fluffy tail and brown eyebrows?"

"And a rebel with tons of attitude. You know Guinness?"

"I know of her. Guinness is my big sister."

WHAT?

I stare at Fury, and I finally see what bothered me all along: the long slick muzzle, the amber eyes, the way he carries his head — all Guinness. All but his frilly golden coat and silly floppy ears.

"Seriously? Are you Fuzzy?"

"I used to be, but Dick didn't think that was an impressive enough K-9 name, so he changed it to Fury."

I shake my head like I'm wet. I can't believe it! He's just like Guinness, but he's not. Guinness is a quintessential German shepherd, while Fury is...I don't know what Fury is.

"I hope you don't mind my asking, but... what breed are you?"

"I'm a golden shepherd."

"Never heard of it."

"It's a new breed, you know, like the cockapoos and the Labradoodles, except we're working dogs. My mom is a German shepherd from champion bloodlines, but my dad's a golden retriever. He's a free dog named Ranger. So, I'm a golden shepherd. Some call us German retrievers, but I don't like that. I'm neither German nor much of a retriever. I'm a shepherd at heart."

I wag my tail. Fury is even less German than Guinness, who's the least Teutonic shepherd I've ever met. He's not much of a retriever either, but he's a damn good-looking dog and quite the K-9 if you ask me.

He cocks his head.

"Would you tell me about Guinness? I so hoped to meet her. Mom and Jones are so proud of her; they never tire of telling stories about her puppyhood. They called her Red, and she was a riot. Jones still has the red sweater she ate a hole in when he left her in the library. He can't bring himself to throw it away."

"Guinness is a character. She always has a unique angle on everything. When she tells you a story, it's like she turns on a flashlight in the dark. Things make sense differently. Guinness is compassionate, hard-working, and funny, but you don't want to get on her wrong side. One time, when she thought I disparaged our friend Butter, she almost ripped open my throat."

Fury's eyes sparkle and his head lifts high.

"Guinness loves popcorn, bacon, and playing with the ball. She's a champion at staring. When we got bored, we held staring contests. Guinness and I stared at each other without blinking until Butter fell asleep. Guinness usually won. Oh, did you know she won NORT?"

"What's NORT?"

"NORT, the National Odor Recognition Test, is like the K-9 sniffing Olympics. The best K-9s compete in finding explosives, firearms, and such. Guinness is the only K-9 I know who even competed in it, let alone win it. Your big sister is an exceptional K-9."

"Oh, how I wish I met her! Where is she?"

"She went home a few months ago."

"Will she come back?"

"I don't think so. When we were on patrol, an insurgent threw a grenade that killed Silver, her handler. Guinness took it badly. This was just weeks after Butter got shot and lost her leg. Guinness had a breakdown, and they sent her home for treatment. Last I knew, she was in rehab, and they were looking to get her a job stateside."

Fury lays his nose on his paws just like Guinness used to do and looks away. He doesn't say anything, but I smell his disappointment.

"I'm sorry, Fury."

He sighs.

"You know, my whole life, I hoped to grow up and be like Guinness. She was my hero. She could do no wrong. So finding out that she lost it and got sent home is a bummer."

My hackles rise, and I bare my teeth to growl and give him a piece of my mind, but I manage to keep my cool. It's not the kid's fault. He just doesn't know any better. He thinks that having a breakdown is something to be ashamed of. But he's wrong.

"Listen, Fury, Guinness is a hero. She's the smartest, strongest, and bravest K-9 I ever worked with, and I'm proud to be her friend. Getting PTSD from this darn war is not her fault, and it's not a sign of weakness. She's nothing to be ashamed of. She's brave, loyal, and resilient. I just hope you grow up to fill her paws someday."

Fury cocks his head.

"You think so?"

"I don't think so. I know so. Guinness is..."

All of a sudden, Sabrina kneels over and hugs me, her eyes full of tears. I don't know what this is about, but I bet it has to do with Dick, and I don't like it one bit. And I HATE being hugged! But I don't want to hurt her feelings, so I hunch there, waiting for her to let go, but she won't.

I break down and lick her face to make her feel better. I'm embarrassed to do this in front of Fury, but he doesn't seem surprised. Isn't that odd? Dick doesn't strike me as the touchy-feely type. Oh well.

I do my best to comfort Sabrina.

"There, there. Take it easy. Everything is going to be OK; you'll see."

She sobs.

"No, it won't. It can't. Viper, I just found out that I'm expecting."

14

Expecting? What is she expecting? Whatever it is, it can't be good. I wonder if it's that MRE we had yesterday. It was even more disgusting than usual. I only had half of it, and I wanted to barf.

I sniff her bottom. She smells a little funky, but she doesn't smell like she pooped recently, which gives me an idea.

"How about pooping? That always helps me feel better. Or at least drink lots of water. That may help you barf."

Sabrina gasps, and I don't know if she's crying or laughing.

"Oh, Viper. That was precious. You almost made me laugh. Thanks for that, I needed it. But this is really serious, you know. I think they'll send me home."

Home? Now that's a thought! I could look for Guinness and Butter. Wouldn't that be a riot if I could track them? As long as Sabrina gets better, I won't miss this dang war one bit. I'll miss Fury, of course. But we won't be gone long, I bet. And I can't wait to have some actual weather for a change, whatever it is, as long as it's not summer in the desert.

"What season is it at home now?"

"It's winter."

"That's totally awesome. I love snow. Do you know how to make snowballs? I love to leap and catch them and then chomp on them. Or we could make Snow Boogeymen we could wrestle into the ground!"

Sabrina's mouth corners turn down, and she starts crying again. I can't imagine why. I was sure she had enough of the heat and the desert.

"Oh, Viper. How I wish we could go back together."

She blows her nose, hugs me once more, and leaves. I stare behind her, wondering what this is all about. She makes no sense whatsoever.

I glance at Fury, who's lying in his crate with his nose on his paws pretending to be asleep, but I see his ears twitching. I bet he didn't miss a single word.

"What the heck was all that? Did she make any sense to you?"

Fury cracks open one eye.

"Viper, you understand what she's expecting?"

"No."

"I thought so. Sabrina's pregnant. She's going to have puppies."

My jaw falls.

"What? Are you out of your mind? How do you know that?"

"I learned it at home, just before I left for training. The neighbor asked Jones why Mom got so big, and he told her she was expecting. She was going to have a new litter."

"But Sabrina can't have puppies!"

"Why not?"

"Well, first of all, she's not a dog. If she had anything, she'd have babies."

"Wow! I didn't think about that. That's even worse."

"You aren't kidding."

I crawl back in my crate to think. I remember Andrew's wife and her vacuum cleaner. I wonder if Sabrina will turn out like that after having babies, harping at everyone about everything. I hope not. But at least we'll get to play in the snow, eat real food, and get rid of the dust. All in all, it sounds worth it.

"I can't wait to play in the snow. I haven't seen snow in years.

Fury glances at me.

"You think you'll go back with her?"

"Why not?"

"You aren't pregnant. And the army is short of explosive detecting K-9s."

"Sabrina won't leave me here. I know she'll take me back with her."

"If she can. But they may not let her."

"But I have nobody to work with."

"They'll get you a new handler."

15

What? My hackles go up. Fury must be wrong! They can't get me a new handler! I belong with Sabrina, and she belongs with me. I can't let her go. Who'd look after her?

But then I remember my other handlers. In the army, handlers are interchangeable, just like K-9s.

Andrew and I trained together and deployed together. I thought we'd be together forever, but he disappeared.

The army gave me George. He was wise, patient, and wifeless, and he taught me most of what I know. But George was old, and he'd already paid his dues to the country, so he retired.

The army passed me on to PJ, who was on his first deployment and thought he knew everything. He reminded me of myself as a pup. I thought I knew it all and hated being told what to do. But by the time I met PJ, I'd learned that staying alive beats looking cool. PJ hadn't.

He strutted down the desert, veering off the track I'd sniffed just to show he was unafraid. The lieutenant talked to him, and PJ nodded, staring at his boots, then did it again. But not for long.

We were looking for explosives in a nearby compound; as usual, I went inside one hut after another, as PJ waited outside to stay safe. I found a box smelling funky, and I called PJ, but he didn't answer. I waited and waited until the locals got restless. So I opened the box, even though that was against the rules. The iffy smell turned out to be just a box of matches, so I went to tell PJ, but he was gone.

I started tracking him when the earth shuddered, and the place went up in flames.

The power of the blast threw me to the ground, and it took me a while to get up, deaf and dazed. I wobbled on shaky legs to look for PJ.

But all I found was his helmet and a damaged boot. The rest was spread over the desert. PJ managed to find the cache of arms protected by the mother of all IEDs, but he didn't get to brag about it.

I was once again without a handler, so the army gave me Sabrina. She had a voice like melted chocolate and magic hands that always found my itchy spots. She brushed me, threw me the ball, and saved the best bits of her MREs just for me.

"You don't have to do that," I said.

"I know. I do it because I love you."

That, right there, was a choker. Nobody had ever told me they loved me. Not my trainers, not Jinx, not even my mother. That's how Sabrina won my heart.

I promised her that nothing bad would come to her while I was around, and I did my best to keep my promise.

But now I'm out of my depth. I'd die for Sabrina if that helped, but I can't fix the trouble she's in. So, I do what I can: I try to be the best friend I can be, I follow her orders, and I struggle to stay awake when she tells me stories. But the danger is looming. I don't know what it is, but it's here. Our time together is almost over. I can smell that like I can smell storms, fear, and explosives, so I do my best to comfort her while I'm here.

16

But nothing happened. Camp life stayed the same: breakfast, patrol, long chats with Fury in the evening, sleep, repeat. I'd have stopped worrying if it weren't for Sabrina fading every day. She woke up tired, fell asleep over breakfast, and puked all the time.

We were walking one morning when she turned white, leaned against a truck, and puked her heart out. I sniffed it carefully. There was no food. No wonder, since she never eats. But there wasn't even grass, wood splinters, or peach pits like I puke when I eat things I shouldn't. Sabrina's barf was nothing but bile.

She dropped on a box, hiding her face in her hands, as Fury and Dick passed by.

Dick's face fell. He came over and touched her shoulder.

"You OK, sweetheart?"

Sabrina shook her head.

"What's going on, baby? Did you eat something that didn't agree with you?"

Sabrina sighed.

"No, Dick. It's not what I ate. I'm pregnant."

"You're what?"

His hand pulled away like she was hot.

"You heard me. I'm pregnant."

Dick blanched. He glanced around at the parked trucks to make sure nobody listened, then cleared his throat.

"Are you saying it's mine?"

Sabrina's cheeks caught fire.

"What do you think?"

He looked away.

"How would I know?"

Her voice stayed low, but I could smell her anger.

"Yes, Dick, it's yours. I haven't dated anyone else since I left home. So, what are you going to do about it?"

"Me? There's nothing I can do. The question is, what are you going to do about it? Did you report it yet?"

"Not yet."

"You should. You want to have enough time to...deal with it."

"Deal with it?"

"Of course. Get rid of it. You aren't thinking of keeping it, are you?"

She jumped to her feet, and he stepped back.

"Dick, do you understand it's a baby we're talking about? Our baby?"

"Sorry, Sabrina, but you have to leave me out of this. You know as well as I do that we aren't supposed to have sex while deployed. We broke the rules. I don't want to get in trouble with the army. And my wife must never find out."

Sabrina stepped back.

"Your wife?"

"Yes. What did you think? I have a wife and three kids. If she finds out, she'll make my life a living hell."

Sabrina wavered and steadied herself against the truck.

"You forgot to mention your wife before."

Dick shrugged.

"You didn't ask."

"I didn't ask. Really. That's all you have to say?"

She turned to leave.

"Let's go, Viper."

Dick grabbed her arm.

"Listen, honey. You've got to be reasonable. The only sensible thing to do is get rid of it. The army will send you back home, where you can get a termination. Quick, safe, and clean. You'll be back in no time. It's so much easier than dealing with a kid for eighteen years. They're a pain in the butt, all of them. And you have no idea how much they cost! The diapers alone...."

Sabrina shook him off, but he didn't let go.

"Come on, Sabrina. You're still young! You have all the time in the world to have kids. And think about what people will say if you keep it! They'll think you got yourself pregnant just to get out of the army, and they'll hate you. But I know that's not true. Or is it? Did you do it to get out of the army? Or did you imagine I was going to propose?"

Sabrina's fists tightened.

"What a loser you are, Dick. Get lost."

"Sorry, Sabrina, I didn't really mean that. You know how much I love you! I'm just in shock. And I'm worried about you. Let's sleep on it, and I'm sure we'll come up with a plan."

Sabrina tried to leave, but he wouldn't let her. His knuckles blanched as he held on to her arm, and she whimpered.

I couldn't take it anymore. I rose my hackles, bared my teeth, and growled, ready to rip off Dick's throat.

"Sabrina told you to get lost. Get lost."

Dick frowned.

"Down, Viper."

I growled louder.

"Are you kidding me? I don't take orders from you, not now nor ever. Get lost, I said."

I was ready to leap when Sabrina pulled me away.

"Let's go, Viper. He's not worth it. Forget it!"

I followed her. But I won't forget.

17

Things got worse after that. Sabrina shrank until you could barely see her from the side, and her brain seemed to drown in a fog. She forgot her vest, she forgot her weapon, she'd even forget me if I didn't keep my eye on her. Sabrina's heart was no longer in her job, and I hated to agree with Dick, but she needed to go home. She knew it too, but she couldn't bring herself to do it.

One evening when Fury and Dick were away, Sabrina brought me her dinner. I refused it since she needed it more than I did, but she insisted. I didn't want to be rude, so I started picking at her so-called meatloaf as she got talking.

"You know, Viper, I'd love to go home. I'm so tired of this war, of the enemy always looking for new ways to kill us, of the blistering heat and the freaking dust choking us. I'm tired of lukewarm water and rehydrated food, and I'd give anything for a bath. But more than anything, I'm worried about what this does to my baby. It can't be good. None of it is good. But I can't bring myself to report and get sent home."

I cocked my head.

"But why? I'd love to go home. You said it's winter."

She sobs, and I shrink. I hate it when she does that. I don't know what to do other than licking her tears, which only makes it worse.

"Oh, Viper. I'd go home in a heartbeat if I could take you with me. But I don't think I can. You're just a few months shy of eight, so you're close to retirement, but you're not there yet. I hope I can last a couple more months, so they let you retire with me. Wouldn't that be wonderful? We could be home together, just you, me, and the baby.

Oops. I forgot about the baby. I'd better keep it in mind since Sabrina seems to have her heart set on it.

I wag my tail in agreement.

"That sounds great. Where would we live?"

I've never lived with Sabrina anywhere but here. I don't know anything about her home. I just hope she doesn't live in Florida. My buddy Rigatoni, a retriever I worked with in Iraq, came from Florida. He said life there revolves around oranges, and I hate oranges. They're almost as rude as lemons if you bite into them. And that's not the worst part. He said that lawns in Florida crawl with alligators; you'd better watch out where you poop if you want to hang on to your assets. They don't have snow, just dust, and I've had enough of that.

"We live in Vermont. Have you been to Vermont?"

"Not yet. Do they have snow?"

Sabrina laughs for the first time in ages.

"Sure, we do. More snow than anywhere but Maine. And New York."

"That sounds good. How about the food?"

"We make the best maple syrup."

Phew.

"That goes on everything, from popcorn to bacon."

Now you're talking. I could live with that, even if it's not healthy food.

"How about organic? Do they do organic?"

"More than anywhere else but California. And they have green mountains and rivers and lakes."

"Sign me up," I say, just to cheer her up. "I'm in. Let's go."

Sabrina sighs, and I smell there's more.

"Viper, you're the main reason I can't bring myself to leave, but not the only one."

I cock my head.

"What else can there be? You said you wanted out of here."

Her eyes avoid mine, and she smells embarrassed.

"It's Dick. I hope...I still hope he'll change his mind."

"About what?"

"About the baby. I hope he comes to want him as much as I do."

Like really? He told you he doesn't want your baby. He already has three of them. And a wife.

"And about me. I know it's not likely. But one can hope, can't we?"

I yawn like we dogs often do when we're stressed. I don't know, girl. Hope is one thing, and reality is another. I'd go with the facts, but what do I know? I've never been pregnant.

I'm still pondering this when Fury crawls in his crate and lays his nose on his paws, smelling troubled.

"What's up, buddy?"

"It's Dick. He's in a state. Ever since he talked to Sabrina, he's been a pain in the butt. You'd think he's the pregnant one."

"I'm sorry."

"Me too. It's a mess. I wonder why humans don't neuter their females before sending them to combat like they do with K-9s. It would be so much easier."

I gasp.

"Like, really? How about the males?"

"Males don't get pregnant."

"Neither do females, without a willing male. It takes two."

Fury glares at me.

"Are you nuts? You're saying they should cut our balls before they send us here?"

"Of course not. But what about the females? What if they feel the same?"

"They can't. Females have no balls."

I don't know what to say. He's technically correct. I've sniffed many butts, and I can't remember a single female having balls. But...

"They must have something, whatever that is. Look at Guinness. And Butter. They're just as ballsy as I am."

"So there. Whatever they take out, females don't miss it. So why not do that to humans too?"

That pisses me off. Fury acts like this is all Sabrina's fault. But I can see where he's coming from. Fury is loyal to Dick, just like I'm devoted to Sabrina, so I try to keep cool.

"Listen, Fury, it's not Sabrina's fault that Dick ignored the rules, forgot his family, and gave in to his instincts."

"But how could he resist? He's just a male."

That makes my blood boil.

"You and I are just males. When was the last time you got anyone pregnant?"

He stares at me like I'm crazy.

"But we're not humans. We're K-9s. That's different."

I've had it.

"Why don't you leave my Sabrina alone and worry about your Dick instead?"

18

Fury turns away without a growl, and I feel terrible. I wish I bit my tongue instead of being rude, but it's too late to unsay it. And it's true. I once almost died chasing love, even though I should have known better. But blood ran hot through my Gallic heart, and I wasn't too old to be stupid.

That was before Guinness when Butter and I were the only K-9s at the base. One night I lay in my crate minding my own business when a burst of wind tickled my nose with the scent of a willing lady of K-9 persuasion.

I thought I was dreaming at first. I was in Kandahar, and I knew damn well there was nothing but desert for hundreds of miles and no dog other than Butter and me. And, as lovely as she is, Butter doesn't give a hoot about sex.

I sniff again. This is no dream. The scent is real. Remote, but clear as a bell. Somewhere in the desert, a lady needs romance, and I have no choice but to go. One can't argue with nature.

I crawl out of my crate, silent as a ghost, and glance around. Butter snores in her crate, and Sabrina plays cards with the men. Nobody sees me as I slip out and run. I reach the fence, and for the first time ever, I wish it was lower, instead of ten feet tall and topped with rolls of razor wire. There's no way I can scale it without getting shredded.

But I can't let this keep me away from my love. I know a tunnel in the back where a couple of insurgents tried to break in last week. We caught them before they finished, so the hole is less than a foot wide, and it's filled with rocks. For the first time ever, I wish I had opposable thumbs rather than my splendid teeth. But it is what it is, so I get digging, and before you can say, "What a good dog!" I squeeze out from the safety of the wire into the desert night to look for love.

I know that's stupid, but my insides burn so hot I don't care. I've done many silly things in my life, and I hope this is not the last.

I rip through the moonlit desert like a silent shadow, following my nose toward my object of desire. And there she is!

My eyes say she's dirty, mangy, and flea-ridden, but my heart tells me she's beautiful. And I'm about to follow my heart when I notice the dozen filthy mutts surrounding the love of my life.

They're mesmerized. Their glowing eyes glued to her, their tongues hanging to their knees, they're too busy to notice me, thank Dog. I step back, ready to flee when the wind changes and they smell me. They turn to me like one, bare their long yellow teeth, and growl.

What happened to love? As soon as they see me, they lose interest in the lady, and I must admit I feel the same. I raise my hackles and growl back, but I know I'm in trouble. I'm alone in the desert with a dozen starved strays who slobber just looking at me.

A big one-eyed mutt licks his lips.

"Hello, Dinner. I've always wondered what infidels taste like. You hungry, boys?"

A tall skinny mutt with his left ear missing drools so hard he chokes when he barks.

"Starved."

"Let's get him," another one calls.

They move to surround me. Their teeth gleam in the moonlight, and their red eyes glare as they leap toward me like a pack of hungry werewolves. For the first time in my life, I'm terrified.

"Stay back, you ugly mutts!" I growl, but they laugh like hyenas and tighten their circle, pushing closer and closer until I give up my pride, turn my tail, and run.

I've never been so humiliated, but I don't have time to worry about my honor. That can wait. What I need now is shelter, and there's none but the base, miles away.

That's not far for a K-9 with my training. I can run like the wind, but I've never fought another dog, let alone a whole pack. I only learned to apprehend humans, whose canines aren't worth mentioning. But these hungry, red-eyed beasts? I've never been in so much trouble.

I might outrun them, but I can't crawl back through that tunnel with them on my tail. They'd rip me apart as I scrambled to squeeze through.

"Take the left, and I'll take the right," One-Eye growls.

"He's ours, boys. The best dinner we've had in weeks," Missin' Ear barks.

I fly across the dark desert with the pack on my tail as I struggle to find a plan before I reach the tunnel. But nothing comes to mind. My heart racing, my brain on fire, I catch the smell of the base. I'm getting close, and I'm running out of time.

I make a right U-turn and leap, landing on One-Eye, who smells even worse than he looks. His one eye widens, showing the white all around it as my teeth tear his throat. I bite deep, like I'm trained to, and taste the salt of his blood as it splashes my face. I drop him and dart forward, hoping his partners will stop to look after him. And they do. The scent of blood excites them to a howling frenzy, and I hear them ripping him as I fly to the base.

Oh boy, that was close. But I'm almost there. I sigh with relief until I see Missin' Ear waiting for me by the tunnel. How the heck did he get here?

His teeth glimmer in the moonlight as he snarls.

"Come on, lover boy. Let's see you crawl in."

His partners' barking gets louder behind me. They're on their way. I only have moments, so I do what I have to do.

I pull my tail between my legs and roll on my back, presenting my belly in submission.

Missin' Ear comes to sniff me like he's supposed to. I wait until he's right above me before I spring to open his throat.

His tortured cries follow me as I squeeze back inside the wire. I stop right behind the tunnel, waiting to kill the first one coming through, but there's no need. They're too busy fighting each other. It feels like forever until Missin' Ear's agonizing screams fade as his friends tear him apart. But for the grace of Dog, that would have been me.

I wait until the silence tells me they're done; then I hobble back to my crate. I'm exhausted, damaged, and humiliated, all in the name of love.

Butter hears me whimper and opens her eyes.

"You OK, Viper?"

"I'm not OK. I'm stupid."

I told her.

She licked my nose, and I felt better.

But I'll never do that again.

19

Still, I shouldn't have been rude to Fury. He turned away, pretending to sleep, but I feel his sadness, and I know he smells mine. Too bad that his loyalty to Dick conflicts with my duty to Sabrina. It's not Fury's fault that Dick is Dick, but Sabrina deserves better.

The following day we both pretended nothing happened, but we knew better. Our devotion to our humans pulled us apart, and our friendship became another casualty of this darn war. We went about our jobs, took turns leading patrol, and watched each other's back, but the unease never vanished. It got even worse when Dick and I got close. I couldn't forgive how he treated Sabrina, and he didn't forget that I threatened him. He couldn't wait to get even.

It was like navigating land mines inside the wire. Sabrina hid her pregnancy, hoping that Dick would change his mind. Dick lived in fear that Sabrina would expose him. Fury was torn between his duty to Dick and our friendship while I struggled to protect Sabrina. We were all stuck with no end in sight.

Until Sabrina fell.

It was a hot morning like they all are in Kandahar. The aerial surveillance blimp had detected unusual activity in a nearby field, so we went to check it out. We filed out as usual: me first, dragging Sabrina on her leash followed by the soldiers, with Fury and Dick in the rear.

I was sniffing underneath a crooked bush when the leash pulled me to a stop. I glanced back to see Sabrina fall in a cloud of dust. My heart skipped a beat when I remembered Silver's death.

But there was no noise. No shots, no grenades, not even a scream. Nothing moved across the desert but a lazy plume of smoke bruising the faded blue sky over the village, far away.

I retraced my steps and sniffed Sabrina. She didn't smell dead. I licked her face, and she opened her eyes.

The men who came to her help looked as confused as I felt. They took her back on a stretcher, and I followed. Fury and Dick led us back.

Sabrina tried to laugh it off.

"It's just the heat. It gets to you. And I didn't drink enough water. I'll be fine by tomorrow."

The lieutenant didn't listen. He shipped her out to get her checked, and I knew her secret was over. That night I lay awake in my crate, wondering if I'd ever see her again.

"Hey, Viper?"

"Yes."

"I hope she's all right. She's a good human. I know you care about her."

"Thanks, Fury."

"What will you do if they send her back?"

"I don't know. I guess the army will assign me another handler."

"Are you worried?"

"About what?"

"About getting another handler. What if you don't like him? What if you don't get along?"

I yawned.

"It doesn't work that way, Fury. Work is work. I'll do my best to get along, and I bet he will too. We're all brothers in arms here. We need to have each other's back."

Fury wagged his tail, but he wagged it left, so I knew he was worried.

What I didn't know, is how right he was.

20

That night and the next day, then another night and another day, I did nothing but waited for Sabrina. I watched the gates, I listened for trucks, I sniffed the wind for her scent.

She didn't come.

I followed her with my mind's eye, willing her to return.

She still didn't.

When my heart felt so empty that I wanted to howl, I stole her socks, and I lay on them to breathe her scent. I was still chewing on them when the lieutenant came to see me.

His eyes avoided mine, so I knew he had bad news.

"Hey, Viper. How're you doing, pal?"

I waved my tail left.

"Fine, thanks. And you?"

"Great. Great. I have a message from Sabrina."

I took a deep breath to slow down my heart.

"Yes."

"Sabrina... she's fine, but she's not coming back. She'll have a baby."

At least she's not dead.

"Viper, Sabrina made a request for you to retire with her, but our rules don't allow for that. You're still healthy, strong, and productive. We can't let you go. And we all know how important your work is to you. You're nowhere near ready to retire. So I put in a request for a new handler. I'm sure you'll work with him just as well as you did with Sabrina."

That's bull, and he knows it. I know it, Fury knows it, even my kibble bowl knows it. But he's got to say something.

"In the meantime, Dick agreed to look after you and train you alongside Fury. Isn't that great?"

Seriously? How thick can you be? How about using your eyes if your nose is blind?

But there's nothing I can do. It is what it is. I can do a few days. Not like I have a choice anyhow. I'll do my best to work with Dick, even though he's the only human I ever hated — besides Jinx's killer, of course. But I never had to work with that one — I only had to bring him to justice. But I digress.

Dick's smirk is hard to take. Now that Sabrina left without spilling the beans, Dick is back to his cocky self, and he can't wait to pay me back for challenging him.

He's good about it, too. He doesn't hit me or scream at me since he knows people would notice. He's a small man, so he does small things: He "forgets" to fill my water bowl, skips adding supplements to my kibble, and fails to let me have my evening walk, so I spend my nights crossing my legs to hold on to my bladder. He watches me squirm, and he smiles.

It drives me nuts, but I tell myself that the new trainer should arrive anytime. I'll be out of Dick's reach before you can say Grass-Fed-Beef-Kibble. I can take a few days. Anyone can take a few days.

Fury sees this, and he's distraught. Like a pal, he shares his water and food with me, but he can't share his bathroom break.

"I'm sorry, Viper. Dick must be troubled by everything that happened, but I'm sure he'll get over it soon. I love you, brother. I'm here for you."

His friendship is the only thing that keeps me sane. I don't know what I'd do without him, and I hope I never find out. With Fury's help, I can take a few days and refrain from tearing Dick's throat. Because I know what happens if I do.

21

I first saw George as I waited for Andrew by the dining room window. He'd been gone for days, but I knew my human wouldn't abandon me like a second-hand bone. He'll be back to get me any moment, I thought.

I was still a pup.

I'd already learned how to deal with explosives and perpetrators, but what I knew about humans could fit in my water bowl with room left over. So, day after day, I sat by the window awaiting Andrew's return.

An old jeep parked in the driveway, and a man in uniform rang the doorbell. I knew he wasn't Andrew or the mailman, but I barked just in case. His gray eyes crinkled in a smile as he took off his cap and ran his fingers through his mop of white hair, waiting for the door to open. He looked up at Mom as she filled the doorway.

"Yes?"

"Good morning, Ma'am. I'm sergeant Whitby. I was sent to collect Viper."

"To collect Viper? What are you talking about? Viper belongs to my husband. Andrew will need him when he returns."

"I'm sorry, ma'am, but my superiors sent me to collect him. Here are the papers. Viper is a working K-9, and he belongs to the army. I'm sure your husband will clarify things when he returns, but for now, Viper belongs with the military."

Mom's eyes glimmered with tears. I wondered why. Not like she liked me — to her, I was just a dirty nuisance. Maybe she also thought that Andrew would come back for me someday?

She brought my leash and handed it to George.

"There."

"Thank you, Ma'am."

Mom slammed the door.

George offered me his hands to sniff. He smelled like hot dogs, sweat, and gunpowder, and I instantly knew I could trust him. I wagged my tail, and he scratched my ears.

"Good to meet you, Viper. You and I will make a good team."

He drove us to a tidy little trailer sitting between dogwood and maple trees, where he let me out to do my business.

I sniffed everything first, of course, but there wasn't much besides George. Squirrels, a couple of stray cats, and some faded dog smells, so old I couldn't tell the breed. What happened to that dog, I wondered? I started exploring, but George called me in.

I checked every inch, of course, but there wasn't much there either. No IEDs, no females, no kids, and no cats, thank goodness. Nothing exciting other than the peppered jerky in the left kitchen drawer.

George laughed and offered me a strip, then put on his glasses to read my papers.

"This is your record, Viper. Good job on your first deployment! You apprehended two suspects, uncovered three IEDs, and found a cache of weapons. No misses that we know of. Not a bad record for a green K-9 with a rookie handler. You miss Andrew?"

I growled.

"Sure, I do. I still can't believe he ran away and left me with Mom. Andrew was my human, the most important person in my world other than Jinx."

George glanced at me above his glasses.

"I'm sorry, Viper, I know it's hard. I know exactly how you feel. I was there too, and I was devastated. But I was too busy to dwell on it, and you will be too."

He shuffled the papers.

"It says here that you and your late brother Jinx were imported from Belgium."

My heart froze.

"My late brother Jinx?"

George sighed.

"You didn't know, did you, Viper? Darn. I'm so sorry. Jinx was put down six months ago."

My stomach turned.

"You're saying Jinx is dead?"

"Yes."

"How?"

George's face darkens as he reads on.

"It says here that Jinx attacked his handler. The man had to shoot him to stay alive."

"What?"

I knew Jinx's trainer. I knew his whole family since that night Jinx and I swapped. They were OK, all but that darn Turbo. How could Jinx attack his human? And why?

"I don't understand."

"Neither do I. The records say that Jinx was an excellent K-9 with no history of aggression. Why would he attack his handler? It makes no sense."

George clears his voice.

"You know Viper, the reason this is in your records is to warn people that someday, for no good reason, you may turn out to be a liability. They're afraid that you're not trustworthy."

Me, not trustworthy? Me? I've always done my job the best I could, ever since I was just a pup. I live for my job. And I'm not trustworthy? My human abandoned me. His wife made my life a pain. Jinx, my twin, died shot by his own handler. And I'm not trustworthy?

This is the worst day of my life. I flatten my ears and lay my nose on my paws, drowning in my misery.

George comes to pet me.

"I'm sorry, Viper. This is terrible. I don't understand it either, but I promise I'll do my best to find out what happened."

I yawn.

"Whatever."

That won't bring back Jinx. Nor my trust in humans.

22

George was right. After we started training, I got too busy to feel sorry for myself. Then we learned we were getting deployed, so finding out about Jinx would have to wait.

But the day before we left, George came home flushed with excitement.

"I've got Jinx's trainer's address. Wanna pay him a visit?"

My heart froze. Jinx's trainer? Could I trust myself to see my brother's killer without tearing his throat?

George felt me.

"Can I trust you, Viper? Will you stay calm and listen?"

"Yes."

"Are you sure? If you attack him, we won't find out anything. And we'll both get in trouble."

"I'll listen," I growled, hoping it was true.

George drove us to Jinx's old home, and my throat tightened. The last time I was here, Jinx and I were just pups. We had our whole lives ahead of us, and everything was fun. Now, Jinx is dead, and I'm here to find out why.

The woman who opens the door looks nothing like the one I remember. Her bright eyes were blue, and she smelled happy. Now they're red, and she reeks of pain. She glances from George to me and steps back.

"Jinx?"

"No, ma'am. I'm not Jinx. I'm his twin, Viper."

She stares at me like she's seen a ghost. George clears his voice.

"Could we speak to you for a moment?"

She lets us in. Everything looks the same but smells different. This house no longer smells like Jinx or his human. I can't even sense the darned cat.

"Thank you for speaking to us, ma'am. We're trying to find out what happened to Jinx. We know he attacked your husband and got shot, but we couldn't find out why. Can you help us?"

The woman shakes her head.

"I don't know. Jinx was the best K-9 we ever had. He was good with the kids, good with me, he was even good with Turbo. He never did anything wrong.

"The day it happened, they went to work as usual. That evening someone called to tell me that Jim and Jinx were on a mission, apprehending a perpetrator, and something went wrong; Jim was in the hospital, and Jinx was dead.

"I thought the perpetrator had shot them both until I found out that my husband was being treated for dog bites, not gunshot wounds. When I asked him, he said that Jinx attacked him, and he had to shoot him. I couldn't believe it.

"Jinx bit you? But why? What did you do?

"Jim told me to leave him alone. I insisted, but he wouldn't answer. He didn't tell the kids either. He just told them that Jinx got shot on a mission. They were heartbroken."

The woman sobs. I know George feels sorry for her. I would, too, if it weren't for Jinx, but we're here to get answers, so I push George to insist.

He sighs.

"I see. Could we speak to your husband to find out?"

The woman looks away.

"I'm afraid you can't. My husband is not here."

"Tomorrow, maybe?"

She sighs.

"I may as well tell you. My husband is dead. He got shot last month on patrol. It looked like an ordinary traffic stop, but the man had a gun and killed him on the spot. Jim didn't even get to draw his weapon."

She wipes her eyes.

"And you know the worst part? I know it in my bones that he'd still be alive if Jinx was with him."

"I'm sorry, Ma'am, I didn't know."

"It's not your fault. It's nobody's fault. But it's hard. I stay awake at night, wondering how to tell the kids. I couldn't bring myself to tell them he's dead; I told them he's on a mission. I looked for some way to tell them that doesn't hurt, but I can't find it. I guess I'll have to tell them anyhow."

"I'm sorry, Ma'am."

George stands to leave. I follow him with a heavy heart. All this, and I still don't know what happened.

I try the woman one more time.

"Is there anyone else who could know? Anyone we could ask? I really need to understand why my brother died."

The woman shakes her head.

"I can't think of anyone."

As I step out the door, I remember:

"What happened to Turbo? Jinx's cat? Where is he?"

The woman bursts into tears.

"He died the same day Jinx did. The evening before, Turbo was chasing squirrels in the driveway when my husband came home. The cat was deaf, so he didn't hear Jim's truck, and my husband ran him over.

"The vet did her best. She watched him overnight, but Turbo got worse, and they had to put him down. I called Jim to tell him, and he flipped. He was terrified to tell Jinx he'd killed Turbo."

23

That's how I know what would happen if I tore out Dick's throat. So, I suck it up, one nasty trick after another, waiting for my new handler. No matter what, he can't be as bad as Dick. Nobody can be as bad as Dick, can they?

Fury and I take turns leading patrol with Dick. Whoever isn't leading brings up the rear with one of the soldiers. But the real work is always in front: sniffing for IEDs, watching for any scent or movement that could mean an ambush, or chasing insurgents.

Today is Fury's turn to lead, and I'm glad to let him have Dick all to himself. Being last is no fun, but I'd rather be as far from Dick as I can.

We file out through the gate. I watch Fury clear the way, and I can barely tell him from the background. His coat blends so well into the orange desert that all I can see is his bulletproof vest and the trail of dust he leaves behind.

He advances smoothly, sniffing his every step. He crosses the open field and reaches the tall mud wall surrounding the village, then follows it along the dry riverbed lined by a bunch of scraggly bushes. That, to me, is the danger zone: That's where Butter got shot, and Silver got killed. There's always some danger lurking behind that cursed wall. Boy, how I hate it. I wish we crushed it into desert dust.

But Fury pushes on, heading toward the open land behind the village where an informant told us the Taliban hid a cache of weapons. That may be true, or it may be just another lie meant to bring us out in the open, where we're vulnerable. We never know.

A few more steps and Fury is out in the open again. Dick follows, then the other soldiers. It's all quiet, and I breathe a sigh of relief. I'm the last to reach the corner when the gunfire blasts, shattering the earth.

I drop to the ground as our soldiers return fire. The hail of bullets raises a cloud of dust so thick I can't even see my paws. My nose burns with the stench of gunpowder, and my ears ring with the clamor of shots. It's like I'm deaf, blind, and nose-blind as I wait with bated breath for the chaos to settle. I don't know what happened to Dick, but more important, I don't know what happened to Fury, and I'm sick with worry.

The gunfire stops, but the ruckus continues. Weapons clang; people scream, groan, and swear; and I still can't see anything but dust. But I smell blood; I just don't know whose it is. I bark.

"Fury! Are you OK?"

"Yep. Waiting for the dust to settle."

I sigh with relief. I'm so glad Fury's OK that I don't even care if Dick is dead or not. But he's not. We have one dead and three wounded, and we still don't know where the fire came from. As far as the eye can see, there's nothing around us but the desert. But the enemy is still here. If they had run away, we'd see the cloud of dust following them. There's nothing, so we know they're sheltered somewhere, waiting for us to move. We're trapped.

The lieutenant shouts.

"Everyone stay put. Let the K-9s go."

24

Now, THIS is what I live for. Apprehending suspects is my thing, even more than finding IEDs. Bombs don't fight back — unless you step on them. But finding and capturing suspects, that's what I love. I love the chase and the fight and the danger. But for all I know, Fury's never done this before. So I bark.

"Fury, wait for me. Don't get going until I'm next to you. Two targets are harder to hit than one. If they divide their fire, we both have a better chance."

"Yep. Thanks, buddy."

"Move as fast as you can, and don't stop. A standing dog is a dead dog."

"Got it."

I slow down my breath as Dan unhooks my leash.

"Go!"

I explode forward, fueled by rage. I fly over the orange field, ignoring the IEDs. Now is the time to take my chances. I hopefully won't find any mines. But if I'm slow, I'm dead. I'd rather risk the IEDs than the bullets.

I hear Fury take off to my left, but I have no time to look back. The gunfire started, and bullets hit the ground behind me like hail.

Fortunately, they're shooting at wherever I was a second ago, and I'm no longer there. A cloud of dust follows me, but everything ahead is clear, and I see where the fire comes from. Not far ahead, there's a divot in the desert. It looks just like a shadow, but there's nothing here to throw a shadow, so I fly to it like the wind. Am I afraid? No time for that.

Just heartbeats later, I see the hole hidden by a dust-covered tarp. It's camouflaged, but the weapon barrels staring at me give it away. I'm flying to it when a burning pain stabs my hip, and I know I've been hit, but I have no time to worry. One last glorious leap, and I land on the tarp. It sinks with me, covering everyone inside. Their weapons fire at the sky, then fall silent as I go do my work, and it's not pretty.

There's three of them under that tarp, all white with fear and unarmed since they crouched to the ground leaving their weapons behind. They scream, call for Allah, and cover their faces while I show them what good behavior looks like. I've never fought three before, so there's some learning, but it turns out you only have to bite one at a time. The other two would love to run and hide, but that's a no-no. There'll be no running and no hiding today.

The joy of victory fills my heart. I'm proud of myself, and I'm happier than I've been in ages as I wait for our soldiers to come and take over. Then a thought crosses my mind, and my heart freezes.

Where's Fury?

Last I knew, he was right behind me. But that was ages ago. Where is he?

I wish I could leave these men and go look for my buddy, but I can't. Every moment I wait for our men to relieve me burns my soul. The insurgents whimper in their corners, covering their bellies and their faces, as I fight the urge to open their throats here and now. I so want to believe that Fury got mislaid and went somewhere else, but I know better.

Our men jump in the hole one after the other and grab the prisoners. I leap out to look for Fury.

I find him halfway back to where we started. He lies on his side, and his breath sprays red into the thirsty dust.

"Fury? Buddy? Are you OK?"

I know that's stupid as soon as I say it, but what else can I ask?

"Yep," he lies.

"What happened?"

He coughs a glob of blood.

"I guess I just wasn't fast enough. I always knew you were faster, but I didn't know you were that fast. Nobody could keep up with you. Next time you should give me a handicap."

He coughs up another blob of blood, and we both know there is no next time. This is it. I should have been a better friend when he was here. I should have been nicer, wiser, and more patient. But I wasn't since I was too busy being a jerk.

My throat tightens, and I struggle to breathe.

"I will. But how about you just run faster?"

His lovely rich tail, so much like Guinness's, slaps the ground, lifting a cloud of dust.

"I'll try, Viper. But there are things one can't do. No matter how good I am, I'll always be a golden shepherd. And no matter how bad you are, you'll always be the Malligator."

I choke, and I hurt. I lick his nose, and it tastes like blood and sorrow.

"Viper?"

"Yes, Fury."

"I need you to do one thing for me."

"What's that?"

"I need you to find Guinness."

"And?"

"Tell her I did my best to be like her. I'm sorry I couldn't. But I tried. And tell her I'm so proud of her. We all are — Mom, Jones, even the freaking neighbors whose cats she chased. I love her, and I so wish we got to meet. But tell her that Mom has another litter, will you? There's got to be a puppy there who hopes to grow up to be like her."

The grief chokes me. I somehow manage to wag my tail.

"Sure. I will. But why don't you do it yourself? You'll get better in no time."

Fury's glazed eyes look at me, and his tail slaps the ground.

"Oh, Viper. You've grown soft in your old age. You've never lied to me before. We both know this is the end for me. Thank you for everything, my friend."

I struggle to say something, but I can't. My throat is too tight. I lick Fury's nose and watch his eyes lose focus as he dies.

"No, Fury. Thank you for being my friend."

25

My heart bleeds as our soldiers lift Fury on a stretcher to take him back to camp. This mission was the deadliest ever. Two dead soldiers, Fury and Josh, and three wounded. We took three prisoners, but we found no weapons. I bet they don't even exist.

The medevac lifts with the wounded, and we file back to camp in mourning silence. I'm first, then Dick, followed by Josh's stretcher and the prisoners. For the last time ever, Fury brings up the rear.

The soldiers drag themselves back, their hearts heavy with loss, but I don't have time to mourn. I must get them back to safety first. The men who ambushed us have pals who can't wait to strike us when we're weak. What holds them back is the fear of killing their own.

My heart races as I skirt the wall, waiting for death to strike. It may be a grenade blowing us up or a hail of bullets mowing us down — you never know. I smell no explosives, but the stench of hate chokes me.

I take step after weary step, but nothing happens as we leave the wall behind and crawl through the desert to the green gates. When they close behind Fury, I finally have time to mourn.

The soldiers cover the bodies with American flags. One after another, we all share thoughts as tears run down dusty cheeks and loyal hearts bleed.

The lieutenant's voice breaks.

"Fury was a brave and loyal K-9. It will be my honor to nominate him for a Purple Heart."

Pimply Dan, a kid who dreams of becoming a K-9 handler someday, sobs.

"Fury gave his life to keep us safe."

"Fury was my loyal partner and my friend," Dick says, and, for a moment, I forget to hate him.

"He saved my life," I say. "I wish I could save his."

Someone carved Fury's name and number on a wooden plate. The lieutenant lays it in our memorial garden, next to Lobo's, Mika's, and other K-9 soldiers who'll never return to serve. Dick kneels to lay Fury's ball and his collar next to it, and that's that.

Fury is gone.

I crawl in my crate to lick my wounds. A bullet grazed my hip, and it burns like the dickens, but that's nothing compared to the grief of Fury's empty crate. His place still smells like him, and the sorrow chokes me. A piece of me died with Fury. I can never be the same again — this war has robbed me of too much. How I hate it! Still, I'll be here until the day I die or until the army lets me go. But where would I go, anyhow?

It's not the first time I've lost a partner and a friend, but what makes it worse is that it's my fault. I told Fury to wait for me to divide the fire, then I flew by him and left him behind since my speed is my strength. The bullet that hit him was meant for me. If he had gone first, would he still be alive? Would the cold body under his flag be mine?

I don't know, but the guilt crushes me. I was Fury's mentor and his friend; it was my job to keep him safe. And I failed.

I lay my nose on my paws, thinking about all the friends I've lost, K-9 and human, and I choke with sorrow. This can't get any worse, I think, when the lieutenant comes to see me.

"You did good work out there, Viper. Thanks to you, we were able to neutralize this enemy unit. Your bravery saved our soldiers' lives. Thank you for your service. I will be honored to nominate you for the Dickin Medal of Valor."

I know he means well, but I couldn't care less about any Dickin' medal. The only thing I care about is Fury, and he's dead. If only....

"But I do have some good news for you. Remember I asked the army for a handler?"

I cock my head. Now that's something. Will I finally get rid of Dick?

"Well, since Fury is no longer with us, Dick needs a K-9 partner. We don't need another handler; we need another whole K-9 team. I already put in a request, but you and Dick will team together from now on. Isn't that great?"

I stare at him in disbelief.

"Are you kidding? You're assigning me to Dick full time?"

"Yes. Isn't that good?"

I fight the urge to puke. This man's so thick he couldn't find his own ice-hole without a funnel.

"Unbelievable."

And I thought it couldn't get any worse.

26

I always thought that depression, like most feelings, only happens to the weak. For a K-9 and a Malinois like me, the only thing that matters is doing your job. Nothing else counts.

But working with Dick changed my mind. Doing my job brings me no pride and no joy.

Though I must admit, he got better. He allows me my evening break and fixes my food like he's supposed to. He even tried an apology of sorts.

"Listen, Viper. I know you love Sabrina. She's a great girl. I'm sorry you thought I was rude to her. That wasn't my intent. I was just trying to make her listen, but I never wanted to hurt her. Or you, for that matter. Let's start over, shall we? We're both stuck here, and it would be better for us both. After all, we share the same purpose: putting the bad guys away to keep the good guys safe."

I look at him like he's dirt because that's what he is. He's a miserable partner, a lousy soldier, and a jerk. He's a sorry excuse for a human: He betrayed his wife, failed the army, and deserted Sabrina. I can't think of a single way he's faithful and worthy. He doesn't even deserve a fight.

"Sure."

I don't trust him. But the fact that Dick is a jerk doesn't preclude me from doing my job, even though it frees me from caring about him. I feel free to ignore his orders, I don't care if he ever gets letters from home, and I have no need to protect him.

The one thing I refuse to do is chase the ball. That used to be my reward for a job well done. The handler throws it, I catch it, and I tug on it a few times to make me feel like I got a live one. That's as fake as tofu burgers, but so what?

So I do my job, but I ignore Dick whenever I can. I watch him throw the ball when we train, and I love seeing his face fall when I look the other way. That feels good, but it's awful. In enemy territory, you need to trust your partners and know they have your back. Dick and I don't, and that's scary. And there's no end in sight.

But one day, the lieutenant comes with good news.

"I have great news, folks. Excellent news, in fact. Our old buddy, Brown, is coming back."

Dick doesn't know Brown, so he couldn't care less, but my heart skips a beat. I jump to my feet.

"Brown? The same Brown?"

The lieutenant nods.

"Yep. The same Brown. I can't wait to see him."

"How about Butter? Is Butter coming?"

I should know better. I knew Butter wouldn't come back since the day I saw her mangled paw. But one can only hope.

"I don't think so. He's bringing a K-9 named Lovely."

Lovely? What sort of name is that for a K-9?

Oh well. At least I'll get some relief. And news of Butter.

27

I wake up every morning hoping today's the day and Brown is coming. I listen for the truck every evening, then I rush to meet it, but there's been no Brown and no dog, Lovely, Ugly, Homely, or other.

But two of our wounded men returned, and we celebrated with MRE desserts. The third one lost a leg and went home.

Many humans wish they were in his shoes. This war has no end, and they'd give a limb to go home.

Dick and I still butt heads. I want nothing to do with him, and he doesn't like me either. But to him, I'm essential equipment, like his gun, his helmet, and his bulletproof vest, so he isn't keen to destroy me. That's why he leaves me alone.

But I miss my friends. I miss Fury, Guinness, Butter, and Sabrina, and my nights are terribly lonely.

I think about them all the time. I remember that night, long ago, when Guinness, Butter, and I talked about the meaning of life.

It had been a terrible day. Carlos, one of our soldiers, shot himself with his gun before dawn.

We woke up thinking we were being attacked. The men jumped from their cots, grabbed their weapons, and ran into position. We searched long and hard. We found no enemy, but we finally found Carlos.

He lay under a truck in a pool of blood, his face a gaping wound. The men tried to revive him, but the thirsty desert had already sucked his blood and his life.

Patrol got canceled, and the men spent the day inside the wire, talking about Carlos and trying to get to terms with what happened.

Matt, Carlos's best friend, stared in the void, smelling guilty. The other men dragged their feet like zombies, their hearts filled with misery. The lieutenant tried to give a pep talk, but he had no pep left either.

Butter and Guinness felt sorry for them, but I didn't. I wasn't sad. I was too angry.

"Why would a healthy soldier kill himself? He had a responsibility and a job to do. He should have gone and killed some Taliban instead of doing their job for them," I growled.

Guinness sighed.

"I guess he didn't want to live anymore."

"But why?"

Guinness cocked her head.

"I dunno. But how about turning this question on its head. What was he living for?"

"Are you kidding me? He had a job to do!"

Guinness's amber eyes gazed inside me.

"Viper, did it ever occur to you that not everyone lives for their job?"

I stared at her.

"What else is there?"

"Lots of things. Friendship, love, and justice, and food, and the good of the planet, and the polar bears, and...."

"Have you lost your mind? The good of the planet? The polar bears? Who cares about the polar bears?"

"I do. I saw a documentary showing how baby polar bears starve to death because the ice melted and their moms can't find food anymore...."

"Come on, Guinness. Carlos didn't kill himself for the polar bears."

"Probably not. But some things in life are more important than doing your job."

I yawned with frustration. I just couldn't listen to that nonsense anymore.

"You're wrong. There's nothing more important than doing your job, I assure you."

"Maybe not to you. But others may think otherwise. Butter?"

"What?"

"What's the most important thing in life for you?"

Butter sighed. She hated to be put on the spot between Guinness and me. The two of us could fight all day and still have some fight left over for tomorrow, but Butter is a Canadian pacifist, and she hates arguing.

"I don't know. Friendship? Love? Loyalty? Feeling that you made a difference?"

Guinness wagged her tail.

"Atta girl, Butter. There, Viper. I rest my case. There's more to life than work."

I'm about to set them straight when Sabrina comes to hug me, and I'm petrified. I hate hugs, especially in public. I'd love to pull away, but I don't want to hurt her feelings, so I hang my head, hoping she'll go away.

But she doesn't.

She hangs onto my neck, sobbing like it's the end of the world, and I ignore her until I can't take it anymore.

"There, there. Everything will be alright. Just wait and see. It's going to be OK."

I lick her tears, and she finally relents.

"Thank you, Viper. I couldn't do this without you. Being with you makes all the difference in the world. I'm so lucky to have you."

She finally leaves as Guinness and Butter exchange glances. They say nothing, but what is there to say?

"That was nothing," I growl.

"Of course."

"She just needed support. She was upset that her buddy died."

They nod, but I know that inside, they're laughing at me. I sigh.

"OK, OK, go ahead. Tell me. What's the most important thing in life? What do we live for?"

"Love? Friendship? Feeling like our lives weren't wasted?" Guinness says.

I can't disagree.

"We live to make a difference. To leave something good that wouldn't be there if it weren't for us," Butter says.

I can't believe I agree with these snowflakes, but there it is. And it's all Sabrina's fault.

"I get it. We live to make a difference and leave the world better than we found it. That's a tall order."

Guinness wags her tail in a dog smile.

"You know, Viper? That's the first time I heard you admit you're wrong."

"Of course it is. I've never been wrong before."

Butter wags her tail and licks my nose. It's been many months, but I can still feel her loving pink tongue, and the grief of my loss explodes in me like a grenade.

I had her, and Guinness, and Sabrina, and Fury. Now all I've got is Dick.

28

By the time I finally caught a whiff of a dog inside the wire, I had lost all hope. I can't tell time, so it feels like forever. We dogs don't have calendars, iPhones, or watches, so we can only tell time by our bellies growling, the days turning into nights, and the change of seasons. That's why whenever you humans return from the bathroom, we act like you've been gone forever.

Anyhow. I'm lying in my crate thinking about Sabrina when the gates screech open and a heavy truck motors in. The sun's down, and the day's almost over. I turn on my other side, trying to sleep. But, just out of habit, I catch a quick sniff. The usual odors tickle my nose: gasoline fumes, engine oil, seriously stale stress sweat. That's got to be the new men. They traveled for days to get here. Then a tantalizing scent drifts by, and my feet hit the ground before I know it. I smelled a dog.

I sniff again. Yep. It's real.

I squeeze between the soldier's legs and dash to the gate. As always, the men rushed to meet the truck because every truck brings hope: An old friend coming back; a letter from Grandma who never learned the internet; a Christmas package from Aunt Rose, who knitted you a pair of gloves, God bless her heart, and sent you her famous fudge. That makes you drool just thinking of it.

Numb after their long travels, the new men shuffle out on stiff legs. Then comes the mail, and then...

She stumbles out of her crate and falls on her face and my heart sings. I just know my life will never be the same. I've never seen anyone so beautiful. I take a moment to catch my breath and get myself together before I introduce myself.

She's compact and furry, with a long, slim muzzle and come-hither eyes that make my knees go soft. She's got cinnamon-colored pancake ears that hang down to her shoulders and shadow her eyes. She blinks, and I'm hooked. I remember having a crush on Guinness, even though she was too busy to notice, but it wasn't like this. Never like this. I'm in love.

"Welcome to Kandahar," I mumble, offering my butt for sniffing, though I know I shouldn't. I'm older, I'm her superior, and I should sniff her butt first. But she's so pretty...

Her little tail quivers a mile a minute as she learns everything about me: what I had for dinner, how I feel about life, and if I'm interested in dating. Oh, boy, am I!

She turns around to let me sniff her, and, right then and there, she breaks my heart. She's spayed. Just like Butter, Guinness, and every other K-9 lady I worked with. Like really? How unfair is that?

I struggle to get myself together and pretend that her being spayed is not my concern.

"Name's Viper. So glad to meet you, Ma'am."

She shakes her head, and her sexy ears float around her head like an aura.

"Call me Lovely, please. I'm no Ma'am, and I expect we're going to be great friends. Are you the real Viper?"

That throws me off. I didn't know there were any fake ones. Oh well.

"I hope so. Why?"

"Would you happen to be acquainted with a Labrador named Butter?"

"Of course. Butter is my dear friend. You know her?"

"Are you kidding? She's my best friend and my mentor. She told me all about you."

I don't like how this sounds. All about me? But why? And especially what?

"Would you care to elaborate?"

"Butter said you're the bravest, most driven, and best K-9 she's ever met. Other than Guinness, of course. She said she never met a K-9 like you. She sends her best regards."

Guinness? Really? Oh well.

"Thank you. I miss Butter terribly. How is she? And where is she?"

Lovely's ears flatten, and she hangs her head, embarrassed to tell me.

"Butter and I had a rocky start. It took us a long time to get close to each other, but I'm glad we did. You know she lost a paw?"

"I do."

"Did you hear about PC? Her Pizza Cutter?"

"No, I didn't."

Nor do I understand what that has to do with Butter. Though she's always been obsessed with food.

"Did she get into cooking?"

Lovely's tail twitches with glee.

"Not really. Butter's more into eating, but that's not what PC is about. That's what she calls her prosthetic paw. She can walk, run, and even jump with it. She became a local hero. Many folks back home look up to her as a role model."

I'm not sure what a Pizza Cutter has to do with being a role model, but I let that pass.

"It sounds great. Let's talk about that sometime. But in the meantime, what if I showed you around?"

She wags her tail, and her little butt wiggles with it. Be still, my heart. I've found the love of my life.

29

I take her around wishing our camp was something exciting like a muddy swamp, a chicken coop, or at least a forest in the fall so we could play in the leaves. But it's not. So I make the most of what I've got and show it to her like it's my kingdom.

"We're inside the wire. That ten-foot wall topped with razor wire keeps us safe from the enemy. In all the years I've been here, nobody got killed inside the wire. Just once, a truck loaded with explosives blew up the gate, but nobody died but the driver."

Lovely raises her pretty muzzle and sniffs toward the wall, but she's unimpressed. So I move on.

"This here is our training area. This is where our handlers hide fake IEDs. They could be anywhere — inside the trucks, under the gravel, or hidden by a piece of debris — and it's our job to find them."

Lovely crinkles her pretty nose and asks:

"Is it always this dusty?"

I gawk at her. Today is as clear a day as I've ever seen here. There are no bullets, no helicopters, not even a dozen people and dogs walking ahead of you to raise dust. But I guess this air takes some getting used to. After all my years here, I don't even notice the dust until it gets obnoxious. This pretty girl will have to learn.

"Of course not." It's usually way worse, I want to say, but I bite my tongue. "It depends. Some days are better than others." But most are way worse.

She wags her tail politely as I struggle to find something else to show her. I can't think of anything pretty, lovely, or even pleasant. This is a remote camp in enemy territory, and the best we can do is survive.

She clears her voice prettily.

"Errm. Where's the grass?"

I cock my head and stare at her.

"The grass?"

"Yes. You know. Where we... empty."

I'm so thick it's not funny. I forgot I used to need grass. That was the cue. But that's like forever ago. And I haven't seen a blade of grass since I arrived in Kandahar.

"We don't do grass here. There isn't much of it. We just let go in the dust."

Her ears perk up, and she stares at me like I'm nuts. Something tells me she's not into dust.

"Are you sure about that?"

Am I sure? You've got to be kidding me. I'm beyond certain. I've been here for most of my life, and I haven't seen a single blade of grass inside the wire. If she were male, I'd tell her to go find out for himself. But she's not. She's the cinnamon-colored lover I never had, and I bite my tongue till it hurts.

"I'm quite sure. But feel free to check and see if you find something better. I'd be delighted if you found a lawn."

She nods and takes off with a new urgency. She's been closed in that crate forever, so she must be looking forward to that grass. She starts sniffing, and I follow her closely. Not because I think there's any chance on earth she'll find grass, but because she's beautiful.

She sprints from the massive trucks to the tall mud fence

covered in Concertina wire and back. I follow, watching her sniff her way. She's pretty good, even though she's stressed by the urgency. But there isn't a single blade of grass in this darn compound, and she grows more disturbed as time goes on.

I'd love to get her grass, but I can't. So, I do my next best.

"I'm sorry, Lovely, but I can't wait anymore. Would you mind if I took a moment behind those tires?"

"Of course not."

"I'll be back in no time."

I run behind the tires and lift my leg like I need to go, but I don't. I haven't had a drink in hours, and this desert sucks the water out of you. But that's not the point. The point is giving Lovely some privacy and a chance to relieve herself.

I try to squeeze something out, watching her with the corner of my eye. She's hiding behind a dusty truck, where she thinks she's safe, but I can still see her squatting in the rearview mirror. I wait until she's done, then I step back like nothing happened.

"I'm sorry it took me so long. Now, do you want to go back to look for grass?"

"I'm good for now, thanks, Viper. How about showing me the living quarters?"

30

I take her inside the massive hangar where the soldiers are celebrating Brown's return. The day Butter got shot was terrible for us all, and they're all delighted to have him back.

Brown's dark face lights up when he sees me.

"Good to see you, Viper. How ya doing, pal?"

"Good, thanks. How about you?"

"Fair to middling. Where's Guinness?"

The lieutenant fills him in.

"She's gone, unfortunately. You didn't hear about Silver?"

"No."

Brown's face falls as he hears the story.

"What a loss. So terrible to hear about Silver. She was a great soldier, and so was Guinness. I never imagined they wouldn't be here when I returned. Where's Sabrina?"

"She's gone too."

Brown pales.

"She got shot too?"

"Nope. She got pregnant."

"Sabrina? She got pregnant here?"

The lieutenant nods.

"But she's OK. She went back home."

"So, who's Viper's handler?"

The lieutenant points to Dick, who reaches his hand to grip Brown's. His knuckles turn white as he tries to show Brown who's tougher.

"Good to have you here. Me and Viper have been the only K-9 team for a while, and it's getting old. It'll be good to have some backup. Would you like me to show you around?"

"No need, thanks. This is my third deployment here, and I don't think much has changed."

"Really? Your third deployment? With this?"

Dick points to Lovely, and my hackles go up. "This?"

Brown's heckles go up, too, though he's got no hair on his neck.

"No. This is Lovely's first deployment."

"Lovely, eh? What a name! But it fits her well. She surely doesn't look like a military K-9."

"Lovely has a great nose, as good as any K-9. She's a springer. They're well known for their tracking ability."

"If you say so. But surely not for their fighting."

Brown smiles.

"Lovely is not here to fight. She's an explosive detecting K-9. That's her assignment, and that's what she'll do. I'll do whatever fighting is needed."

Brown's hard eyes look Dick up and down. He's already taken his measure, and I can smell he likes him just as much as I do.

Isn't life interesting!

31

Today is Lovely's first mission outside the wire, and it's a scorcher.

Patrolling around the base isn't hard once you learn the ropes. I'm not saying it's easy, but if you take your time and pay attention, you'll be all right more often than not. And if something's fishy, you can abort and return to base. Mishaps may happen, but if you're vigilant, you retain some control.

But that's not today's mission. We're driving to man a highway checkpoint miles away.

Our informers told us that the Taliban expects a massive load of explosives coming over the Kabul-Kandahar highway. We don't know when, we don't know what, we don't know how. We just know that this load means hundreds of IEDs to kill our men if we miss it.

If that's true, of course. Half of our informers work for the Taliban, and they feed us loads of poppycock to bring us out in the open where they can hurt us.

At the checkpoint, you're a sitting duck, miles away from the base, out in the open where everyone can see you. You're stuck there for hours to check whatever's coming, and every truck, car, or bike could be a bomb aimed at you. And by the time you sniff it, you're up with the angels.

I don't like it one bit, but nobody asked for my opinion. And what I like the least is that this is Lovely's first mission. She hasn't been outside the wire yet, and she wouldn't be here today, but Dick made a fuss.

"I've been outside the wire every freaking day for weeks. And now you've got this suicide mission, and you want me to go alone? How about the other K-9s? They've been here for weeks, sitting on their assets. It's high time they did something besides trimming their nails."

The lieutenant was torn. Dick was right, but this wasn't a mission for a rookie. Lovely should have been out patrolling, but like everyone else, the lieutenant succumbed to her charm. He tried to give her time to adjust and kept her safe for as long as he could.

"But they've never been outside the wire, and this is not a mission for a rookie."

Dick snickered.

"And whose fault is that?"

The lieutenant shrugged.

"OK then. You all go. Stay safe."

Fat chance.

The rising sun drips blood over the desert as we load into the massive army trucks to ride to the checkpoint. A wailing song cries through the air from the nearby compound. I've heard it so many times I don't notice it anymore, but Lovely jumps to her feet, and I remember how my insides used to twist in knots every time I heard it.

"What's that?"

"It's the Muslim call to prayer. It happens five times a day. Nothing to worry about."

Lovely shivers, even though the desert wind is hot, and sniffs the air like she wants to smell the song.

I lick her nose.

"Listen, baby. There are plenty of things to worry about down here, but that ain't one of them. Wipe it off your radar. Listen for firearms, detonators, steps, voices, even for the silence. But the call to prayer is not your problem. It's just a distraction you need to ignore."

She slows down her breath and forces herself to calm down.

"Thanks, Viper. Anything else I should know?"

Oh, boy. Where should I start? I wish I didn't have to start today, but here we are.

"That checkpoint? It's a trap. We'll be like sitting ducks there, waiting for someone to take us out. This whole thing about the explosives transport is likely a hoax to get us away from the safety of the base and blow us to high heaven. The enemy hates K-9s even more than they hate our soldiers. They'd give anything to see us dead because we are so good at what we do."

"Who does?"

"Everyone."

"So, what can I do?"

Good question. I've done it for so long I don't remember. It's like swimming. It's easy to do but hard to explain.

"The first thing you should do today is to sniff for people rather than explosives."

Lovely cocks her pretty head.

"What do you mean? I was trained to sniff for explosives, not people!"

"That's exactly what you'll do when we're on patrol. You'll check every inch of the desert for IEDs, and that's going to keep us all alive. But this mission is different. The would-be suicidal bombers, whether they walk, ride a motorcycle, or drive a truck, they're so amped up they stink like stress. They sweat bullets, hoping to get close enough to destroy us when they kill themselves. That's why you need to keep away."

"But then, how can I detect explosives and point them out?"

"That's just the point. When the air reeks of hate, dread, and fear, point that to your handler, whether you smell explosives or not. It's their job to sort it out. Don't get near anyone who smells like they're ready to take off to heaven and want you with them."

Lovely's brown eyes look at me like I'm God, and my heart melts. I wish I could keep her out of danger, but I can't. Dick can't wait to get Brown in trouble, and there's nothing I can do.

"Thanks, Viper. I'll do the best I can."

"I know you'll do great."

My heart sinks. I wish I wasn't lying.

32

Lovely and I sit shoulder to shoulder as the truck rattles our brains all the way to the checkpoint. The darn thing is just a massive cube of filthy concrete by the roadside, broken by wide openings letting the wind through. As well as the dust, the heat, and the bullets.

Lovely yawns. I smell her worry, and I know she senses mine. This no man's land in the middle of the desert is tricky, and we all know it. The soldiers' faces shine with sweat as they raise their hands to stop the vehicles. They're all kitted in bulletproof vests and helmets, and they buckle under the weight of equipment, weapons, and ammo. I can't see their eyes since they all wear dark glasses, but I can smell their fear as they wonder where death's coming from.

Their job is to stop the cars; Lovely's and mine is to find the danger. We divide into teams, and we each take one direction of Afghanistan's deadliest road.

I sniff under cars, check people, and keep track of everyone's sweat. I watch the desert for any movement that might mean badness coming our way. I also watch Lovely and everything that heads her way, so I'm plenty busy without worrying about Dick's rage.

I thought he'd be glad to have Brown and Lovely here for this dangerous mission, but it turns out he's not. He watches them with a nasty frown. Deep inside, he wants them to fail.

Oh well. Dick will be Dick.

I wriggle under a rusty car to check the chassis, struggling to ignore the dust. There's nothing here. I crawl out and stick my head in the window to sniff inside. There are two men and a goat, and they smell OK other than needing a shower.

Dick glares at them.

"Where are you going?"

"Suq. Market."

The goat bleats in agreement.

Dick glares at her, and she stares back. He lets them go and moves to the scooter behind them. Two men and two little kids squeeze together on a tiny scooter, their shalwars swelling in the wind, their sunburned faces split by white grins.

"Where are you going?"

"Al'usra."

"To visit family," Abdul says. Our translator is a slight man in combat fatigues with a soft voice and weary eyes glancing back often. And for good reasons: The translators are the only targets the Taliban hate more than they hate K-9s. To them, they're traitors. They'll stop at nothing to make an example of them and their families.

I sniff the scooter. The four smell alright. Better than that, in fact: they smell like mantu — steamed dumplings with yogurt, mint, and garlic.

I swallow my drool and glance across the road.

Lovely crawls under a massive truck. Sniff-sniff-sniff. Sniff-sniff-sniff. She moves slowly but smoothly, checking every inch, and I'm proud of her.

Dick isn't. He spits to the side and mumbles.

"Just take all day, will you? After all, you only have two more vehicles waiting."

Usually, we'd help them clear the load, but not today. Dick watches Brown lift Lovely in the massive truck and frowns:

"Like, really? You call that a working K-9?"

I'm about to add that to my list of grievances against Dick when I sense something funky.

It's just a plume of dust heading down the road toward us, but it moves too fast. My hackles go up. I signal Dick, but he's too busy hating on Brown to notice. I have to bark twice before he turns to me.

"What?"

The blue car heads toward us at full speed, and I know my instinct was right. I bark to draw Brown's attention as Dick takes out his weapon.

"Stop!"

The car shoots forward as if it wants to meet the hail of bullets flying toward it. The quiet dusty road explodes into a cacophony of gunfire, groaning engines, and screams. Just heartbeats later, the car plows into the massive truck Lovely was checking and bursts into a fireball spitting shrapnel. The world disappears in a cloud of dust, stinking like death. The air's too thick to breathe, so the soldiers cough, scream, and choke. And so do I. There's so much noise my ears hurt, but I don't hear Lovely.

I have to find her.

The smoke's so dense I can hardly see, but I leap into the burning truck to look for her. There are three dead bodies, none of them hers. I jump out as the truck blows up. The blast throws me to the ground, and the world goes dark.

I open my eyes, wobbly and dazed. I shake my head to clear it and look around for Lovely, but I can't see her. Down the road, our soldiers brave the dust struggling to regroup, but she's not there either. I call her, but she doesn't answer.

My heart freezes. Lovely can't be gone. Not the love of my life! That can't be!

I check behind the truck. I sniff inside the concrete cube. I race up and down the road, calling her. Nothing.

That can't be. I can't lose her. I just can't.

My voice breaks as I bark for her one more time.

"Lovely? Where are you?"

"Viper?"

Thank Dog, she's here, right behind me. She's a bit dusty, but she's just as petite, soft, and lovely as ever. And she looks unscathed. My heart melts.

"Lovely!"

"Viper? Are you hurt?"

Hurt? I taste the blood in my mouth, and I feel my paws burning. I guess I am, but I didn't notice.

"Just a scratch. How are you, Lovely?"

"I'm good. Let's look for Brown."

We head back to the burning mess of tangled metal, burning tires, and body parts scattered between the screaming wounded. There are debris, blood, and guts, but there's no Brown.

"He isn't here."

"He was here a moment ago. He pulled me out of the truck when you warned us, and we took cover. Then the world exploded, and I lost him."

We keep looking, though we can barely see or smell anything but the burning mess.

"Sorry, Lovely. I'm afraid...."

"Absolutely not. I know Brown's alive. He was just here."

I feel sorry for her and for Brown. He was a good man.

"Lovely, I'm..."

She won't even listen. She rushes to sniff one body after another, then makes a beeline to the ditch behind the truck. I follow her.

"Brown!"

Sure enough, it's him.

33

Bloodied and covered in dust, Brown kneels over Dick, struggling to breathe life into him. He compresses his chest again and again, then starts over.

But Dick is beyond this. Even if you can't smell he's dead, his frozen blue eyes and the gaping wound in his neck tell the story.

"Come on, Brown. He's dead. And we will be too if we don't get out of here," I bark.

Brown sighs.

"You're right. They must have heard this explosion from Helmand. Any loser with a Kalashnikov within a hundred miles will rush here to finish what his friends have started. Let's go."

We join the rest of the soldiers, and I'm glad to see they're all alive. But Abdul is in trouble. His left hand hangs by the skin, so Brown helps Dan tie a tourniquet to stop the bleeding, as the soldiers burn a purple flare to get the medevac. We're all scratched, bruised, and shaken, but we're lucky to be alive. That car must be scattered over half of Kandahar. The men in the truck didn't make it. Nor did the grinning kids on the scooter.

We wait until the helicopter takes Abdul before we load back in the truck and suffer through the long trip back in mourning silence.

I managed to stay alive through another bloody mission. So did Lovely and Brown. But Dick didn't make it, which makes me sad, even though he wasn't my friend.

The sky is blood-red as we reach the base at dusk. We drag ourselves back inside, all too tired to talk. But the army says we must have a debriefing, so the lieutenant tries to engage the men and give them hope. He'd fare better if he didn't smell hopeless too.

Brown checks Lovely all over, then cleans up my wounds and covers my blistered paws with soothing ointment.

"Not bad, Viper. The wound on the hip is just a scratch, and the paws will heal in no time. Let me see your mouth."

My mouth's still bleeding since I pulled the truck door open with my teeth when looking for Lovely. I loosened a tooth and bit my tongue.

Brown cleans me up and pushes the tooth back in place. It hurts like heck and it still feels loose, but he does his best to anchor it to its neighbors with wire and glue.

"If I were you, Viper, I wouldn't try for any beauty contests right now. But you should be all right if you keep your mouth shut."

I cock my head.

"Are you nuts? I can't keep my mouth shut."

"There's that."

He pats my back and brings our dinner before attending his debriefing. I'm hungry, but my mouth hurts, and I don't feel like eating, so I lay my nose on my paws to think.

Dick died. It was his own fault, even though I won't tell anyone. We, brothers in arms, stick together even if we hate each other. If you rat on someone, you're a snitch, and people no longer trust you, even when you tell the truth. But Dick is dead, and he won't come back to torment me. I should feel happy, but I'm not.

I feel sad, tired, and old. Today's ordeal aged me, and its memory will stay with me forever. I'll never forget those two grinning kids on the scooter who smelled like mint and garlic. Their family must be waiting for them. I'm glad I won't be there when they get the news.

I'll never forget Abdul's ashen face nor his hand hanging by its skin, nor Dick's frozen blue eyes. His wife and his kids don't know yet, but they will soon. What a terrible waste.

I try to think about something happy, but nothing comes to mind. All I can think about is death, loss, and disaster.

"Viper?"

"Yes, Lovely?"

"To me, you are the most handsome K-9 ever, broken tooth or not."

Really? I gaze into her chocolate eyes, I see her tail quivering, and my heart melts. Maybe I'm not so old after all?

"I was so scared, and you were so brave. I lay in that ditch paralyzed with fear. Then I saw you jump in the burning truck to look for me. That gave me courage. Thank you for saving me."

Well then. I didn't really do anything. But I'd be a fool to throw away the credit. So I sigh like I'm about to expire, and I do my best to look exhausted, brave, and heroic.

"I'd die for you," I say. And, as corny as that sounds, it's true.

Lovely crawls in my crate. I move aside to make room for her. I've never shared a cage before, but it's not bad. She lays her pretty head next to mine, and my insides melt.

She licks my nose and says:

"Let's hope that won't be necessary."

I lick her nose, and I forget about everything else. For the first time in forever, I don't feel alone.

Hope blooms as I lie next to my Lovely and listen to her heartbeat.

34

Falling in love is magic. It's like all these years of muddling through, striving to stay alive, washed off my back. My scars, my aches, even my nightmares vanished. I feel young, strong, and hopeful, and I've got a new spring in my step. Even the dust tastes better when I share it with my love.

I know it's not real, of course. I'm not an idiot. I'm almost eight, and I've seen more death and loss than most soldiers, K-9 or human, but it's terrific to dream. It's like watching a movie or listening to a story. I haven't done much of either, but Guinness told me about it.

After Butter got shot, we were so broken that we lay in our crates, talking about anything but Butter. I told Guinness about Jinx and his cat; she told me about the movies she loved to watch.

"You know it's not real because you can still smell the stinky library carpet as you watch border collies herd sheep over green meadows, but it still does your heart good. You escape your surroundings to live in your brain. It's like dreaming, but you're awake. They call it suspension of disbelief."

"Where did you learn all that?"

"At home, watching movies with Jones. Then with Silver. You've never watched a movie?"

I shake my head.

"In Belgium, we lived in the kennel. Then, when Jinx and I came over, we got assigned to the army kennels, and we had no movie night. We barely had bathroom privileges."

Guinness cocks her head.

"But you lived in your handler's home, didn't you? Didn't your family watch movies?"

"I don't know. Mom didn't like me in the living room. She said I shed like an animal, so she kept my crate in the mudroom. I stayed there unless Andrew took me out. He often did, just to get away from her."

"That explains a lot."

I wonder if I should feel insulted.

"What do you mean by that?"

"Have you ever been in a loving home, Viper? A place where you can relax and feel safe? Where you don't have to sniff for bombs, don't have to talk unless you want to, and you feel comfortable and loved?"

I shake my head.

"Never. You mean just lie there without worrying about orders, or shedding, or bombs?"

"Yep. You stretch out to sleep. You can even lie on your back if you feel like it because no one will ever hurt you."

"Nope."

Guinness sighed.

"You know, Viper, I never realized how lucky I was. I've had not one but three loving homes where I never had to worry. I was always loved with Mom and Jones, even when I ate Jones's boots and puked them all over the kitchen. Mom cleaned up after me, so I never had to face the music. Then I moved with Shorty, who taught me to dig for clams, listen to country music, and drink beer. He also taught me about unconditional love. I was heartbroken when he died, but then Silver opened her heart to me. I'm one lucky dog."

I don't get it. My life has always been my job. Guinness is only half my age but has so much to teach me.

"I can't wait to go home. Silver and I will go for long hikes in the woods, we'll eat popcorn, and we'll watch our favorite movies: *Homeward Bound*, *Old Yeller*, and *Babe*. Even *The Art of Racing in the Rain*, though that's nonsense. No self-respecting K-9 would want to drive a car rather than run. That movie is weak on the specifics, but it hits you in the feels. I almost cried when I watched it."

I cocked my head.

"You didn't. You couldn't have. Dogs don't cry."

Guinness shook her head.

"Oh, Viper. You have so much to learn."

I remember her voice, her scent, and the sadness in her golden eyes, and my heart tightens. Oh, how I miss her! That was just days before Silver got shot and Guinness...

Lovely lifts her pretty head.

"What's up, Viper? Everything OK?"

Her voice brings me back to here and now. I'm a lucky dog. I'm happier than I've ever been. With Lovely by my side, I'm ready to take on the world. So why the heck are my eyes watering? Dogs don't cry.

"I'm great, Lovely. How about you?"

"I'm wonderful. Just wonderful."

She lies back, and I rest my muzzle on her shoulder, remembering Guinness.

"Oh, Viper, you have so much to learn."

Damn you, Guinness.

Why do you always have to be right?

35

Those were the days! Lovely and I were always together. Brown trained us both, and we challenged each other to find the fake IEDs he hid for us. Whoever found them first got a treat. Lovely loves food, but my favorite treat, as always, is the ball. Brown throws it, I fetch it, he gives it a few tugs, and it's all worth it.

At night, Lovely and I lie next to each other, talking about everything under the stars. I tell her about Belgium, but it's not much since I was too young to remember. She tells me about Butter.

"We didn't get along at the beginning since she was so bitter."

My jaw drops.

"Butter, bitter? You've got to be kidding! Butter is a Labrador! She's the sweetest K-9 I ever met."

"Really? There, see this? Butter did it."

Lovely shows me a three-inch-long jagged scar along her neck, and I'm flabbergasted.

"Butter? But why? I've never even seen her mad."

"Lucky you. But to be honest, I deserved it."

"What did you do?"

"I took away something important to Butter."

"What?"

"Her self-respect."

I cock my head, trying to understand, but Lovely is done.

"Enough about that. Just remember that when you take away somebody's treasure, even the meekest person can become a killer."

I don't see how that's news, but OK. I'm about to fall asleep when I hear boot steps around me, and my hackles go up in a panic. The last time that happened, they tried to give me a bath. I had to fight for dear life. I thought they'd learned their lesson, but there they are again. I jump to my feet, looking to escape when they start singing.

"Happy birthday to you,
Happy birthday to you,
Happy birthday, dear Viper,
Happy birthday to you."

It's my birthday? Really? Why didn't anyone tell me?

The lieutenant sets an MRE birthday cake in front of me, and it's the ugliest thing I've ever seen, but the aroma makes me slobber. It's a slice of rehydrated meatloaf frosted with ketchup and sprinkled with cheese cracker crumbs with a burning match instead of a candle.

The lieutenant blows off the match, and I inhale the cake and the match before I remember to leave some for Lovely. Oh well.

"Happy Birthday to Viper, our veteran. Thank you for your hard work and all the lives you saved."

I wish I had something to say, but I don't. So, I wag my tail in thanks.

"Good cake. Thanks."

They clap their hands, Brown scratches my ears, and Lovely licks my nose. Life is good.

Then I hear the gates screech open.

"They finally arrived," the lieutenant says, and they all rush to the truck. Lovely and I follow.

"Who?" I ask.

"The new K-9s."

36

My heart skips a beat.

The new K-9s? What new K-9s? Why did no one tell me?

I dash through the door and run to the truck, and Lovely follows. I sniff so hard that I sneeze, but other than the dust, I only smell a hot engine, gasoline fumes, and men in dire need of a shower.

"Lovely, do you get anything?"

She sniffs her heart out.

"It's a male. But I can't tell the breed."

Seriously? Lovely smelled him before me? My male pride gets seriously wrinkled, but I manage to act like I knew it all along.

I keep sniffing until I catch a whiff, and I'll be darned if she's not right. That makes me look at her with new respect. She may be female, small, and cute, but her nose is excellent. Even better than mine.

We sit shoulder to shoulder, waiting for the new K-9, and watch the newcomers scramble out on stiff legs, numb after long hours of travel.

"Did you know anything about this?" I ask.

"No. But I felt something. There was like a stir in the air."

She's right. I feel it too. It's like when you sense a storm brewing, even if you don't know how. Your skin tingles, your ears get itchy, and your stomach stirs. I feel this new dog will change everything, and I'm sick with worry. We're usually excited to get new K-9s because they share the work and bring color to our social life. But not today.

The crate door creaks open, and the ugliest dog I've ever seen jumps off the truck to faceplant in the dust. The poor guy's so ugly that I can't tell his breed or even color. I only know what he's not. He's not a Malinois, nor a Labrador or a German shepherd. Not even a springer. He's sturdy and compact, with sharp ears and a coat the color of burned toast and crummy weather.

Lovely cocks her head in wonder.

"What is that? Is it a hyena?" she whispers.

"I don't think so. It's got to be the new K-9," I reply, observant as usual.

"He's different."

"Yep. Interesting."

That was Andrew's rescue word. He never said he hated something, whether it was the food, the weather, or Mom's new haircut. Whenever he disliked something, he called it interesting.

But, interesting or not, this is our new buddy, so we step forward to introduce ourselves.

"Hi, buddy. I'm Viper. This is Lovely."

"Glad to meet you, guys. I'm Rambo."

He wags his tail and perks his black ears. His hazel eyes are kinda glazed, and that's no wonder since he's been traveling forever and he just landed on his head. But he seems friendly enough as he turns politely to offer us his butt. He's tired and thirsty, and he could do with some food, but other than that, he's OK.

We offer our butts to reciprocate. Rambo sniffs Lovely with more interest than I care for, then gives me a cursory check and wags his tail. We turn around to chat.

"Where are you from, Rambo?"

"Iowa."

"Originally?"

"Oh. I'm Dutch."

"Really. I'm Belgian."

"I know."

He wags his tail left, and I know exactly what he's thinking. Our countries are neighbors, but the Dutch believe they are superior. There's this old joke: Whenever a Southern Dutch moves to Belgium, the average IQ of both countries goes up. That's nonsense, of course, but there's your Dutch mentality. I'll have to nip that in the bud.

Lovely seems mesmerized.

"Are you a Dutch shepherd?"

"Of course."

"Wow! I never met one before."

She stares at him like he's unique, and I wish she weren't meeting one now.

"We're quite rare," he says modestly.

I refrain from baring my teeth.

"What color are you, if you don't mind my asking?"

"I'm brindle. We all are."

"Brindle!" Lovely steps closer to check his coat like she's looking to buy it.

"I'm a golden brindle. Some of us are silver. But we all have to be striped. It's a breed requirement."

"What a stupid thing. Like the color makes any difference. We Malinois can be any color we want. It's what's inside that matters."

Rambo gives me a side glance but keeps his mouth shut.

Lovely doesn't. She glares at me.

"Viper, you always have something interesting to say."

I think she just called me stupid.

37

I spent that night alone in my crate. Gone are the nights when Lovely and I lay with our bodies touching. Now, she doesn't even look at me, and I'm heartbroken.

I thought we had something real, something different, something unbreakable. And all it took to break us apart was this ugly stranger. I don't get it.

I listen to her breath and sniff to read her feelings. But there are no feelings. She's snoring like a chainsaw while I toss and turn. On Lovely's other side, Rambo's crate is quiet. He traveled for days, and now he sleeps like he'll never wake up. If only.

The morning finds me raw and restless. I'm so ready to show this intruder what's what that I shake with excitement. I've been here for years while he just arrived, so I hold the home advantage. I look forward to showing Lovely who's the best K-9, even though the sleepless night and the worry didn't do much for me.

We head out for our morning walk with Brown and Ashley, Rambo's handler. She's a slight blonde girl with a narrow face and bright blue eyes who looks too young to be here. This has to be their first assignment, so I decide to show off.

"This is where we train, and our handlers hide fake IEDs for us to find."

Rambo wags his tail like he doesn't care, so I proceed with my lecture.

"They're not active, of course. It's just about perceiving the smell and signaling it to the handler. We do that by sitting next to it. We don't paw at it, we don't bite it, we don't try to dig it out."

"Yep."

"I'll show you."

I take off like an arrow, looking for the decoy I know Brown hid somewhere. I saunter down the field, doing my best to look sleek, macho and *vaillant.*.

I watch for Lovely's eyes to stay glued to me, but they aren't. She's fascinated with this ugly Dutch, even though he doesn't do much to entice her.

I swallow my bile and push on until I hear Rambo clear his throat.

"Hey, Viper?"

"Yes?"

"If I were you, I'd check the left rear wheel of the truck you just passed. It might hold something interesting."

I take a deep breath to slow down my heart. I have never, ever, in my entire career missed an IED. That I know of. That can't be true. But I have to check if only to dismiss it, so I retrace my steps.

Sure enough, there's a decoy just where he said it was, even though he never went near it. My heart pummels, and my head is about to blow up in smoke. But he's right, and you can't argue with right.

"You're right. Thanks, Rambo."

"No worries."

I keep myself from glancing at Lovely. I used to be her hero, and now I'm what? I don't want to know. The bile in my throat flows thick and bitter as I sit back, letting the others have a go. To say that I'm embarrassed doesn't start to cover it.

I watch Lovely go through her turn flawlessly, albeit a bit slow. Her legs are half the length of mine, so she's got to hustle, but she finds the fake IED hidden in the back of the rusty truck and sits next to it, her tail quivering with joy.

"Good job, Lovely."

Brown rewards her with a treat, then we fall back to watch the newcomers. This is our home. I've gone through it a thousand times, and I know every inch of this place. I've smelled the dust; I know the shadows on the ground; I've sniffed every rusty screw in those trucks. But Rambo and Ash haven't been here before, and they have to learn.

"Go."

Rambo heads out, sniffing his steps like a smelling machine. "Sniff-sniff-sniff. Sniff-sniff-sniff." He moves slowly, but he never stops. I remember Guinness: "Slow is smooth, and smooth is fast." Rambo is smoother than any K-9 I've worked with. His sturdy brindle body moves like the energizer bunny clearing up the yard.

He seems ready to jump in the next truck, but he doesn't. He gives it a couple good sniffs and goes down his way to the next one. He stops and sits next to nothing.

Has he lost it?

Apparently not. Ash throws him his Kong, and he catches it in mid-air, then he gets a good tug while I still wonder what this is all about.

Ash digs out a few matches buried half a foot into the ground, and Rambo goes crazy licking her face.

"Good job, boy. Good job, Rambo."

She pets his ears and kisses his black muzzle, and he doesn't seem to mind. I'm horrified. What kind of relationship is that?

He wags his tail.

"You guys ready for lunch?"

Lovely stares at him like he hung the moon.

"That was fantastic. Totally amazing. Where did you learn to work the terrain like that?"

"Here and there. It's no big deal. It's all about paying attention and not getting distracted."

That's a jab in my ribs, and I deserve it. I screwed up. I'm lucky it was just a decoy. If it were real, we could all be dead.

"No, seriously. Is this your first deployment?"

Rambo's tail wags as he tries to pacify me.

"Not exactly. I've been in minefields before."

"How so? And where?"

"Have you heard about Princess Di's work on land mines?"

"Who's Princess Di?"

"Never mind. I spent some time demining in Angola a while back. Then I went to Cambodia for a stint. I loved it there. Asian food beats MREs every time. And a few other places. So, even though this is technically my first deployment, I've been around a little, and it helps."

I hung my head. What's most humbling is that he's not even trying to humiliate me. He's just matter-of-fact as my liver smolders.

"Nice job, Rambo," Lovely says, squeezing close to him.

Females!

38

That was just the beginning. This ugly stranger's arrival turned my life upside down. I used to think I was the best K-9 ever, but for Jinx. And I was right.

Now, watching this hyena-like intruder showing me what's what burns my guts. He's young, strong, and fast. His hips don't ache, his eyes don't tear, and he doesn't have seven years' worth of desert dust lining his lungs. He's smooth and unflappable, and he's not even a jerk so I can hate him openly. Lovely looks at him like she used to look at me, and he doesn't mind one bit.

Never mind. I'll just have to work harder. Soon enough, she'll get bored with him and remember who saved her life.

A few days later, when we go on a mission, I'm glad I'm leading. The aerial surveillance recorded someone hiding something in a hole a few miles down the road. We don't know what, but whether it's weapons or explosives, we need to find them.

It's my time to shine. Brown fits my bulletproof vest and clips my leash.

"Be careful, Viper," Lovely barks.

I wag my tail and head to the gate, followed by Brown and the others. Lovely and Dan are in the middle, and Rambo closes the file with Ash.

The gates open, and I step out. It's still early morning, and the glowing red sun has painted the desert into a sea of blood. It's just like when Dick died, and my heart skips a beat. Is this an omen?

I wonder if that's how Butter felt the day she got shot; or Guinness, the day she lost her mind; or Fury, the day he died. It's hard to explain how we dogs feel things. The foreboding engulfs you like smoke. It's not just in your nose; it's everywhere. Your skin crawls, your throat tightens, your stomach roils, and your heart freezes. You sense danger with all your body, and I've never felt it stronger than today.

Oh well. It is what it is.

I sniff my way to the field, and the others follow. The earth is already hot under my paws, and I'd love me some shade, but there's nothing here to give shade but us.

Once in the field, we're out in the open. Nothing stirs the dust as far as the eye can see. Nothing moves, but the smoke marring the pale sky far away, over the village. The soldiers hold their arms ready as we spread to comb the field.

I sniff something to my right. I track it, and sure enough, I find the place where the earth was disturbed. It smells funny, so I sit next to it.

Brown kneels to finger-sweep the sand, looking for the pressure plate but doesn't find it. He calls back.

"There's something here, but it doesn't look like an IED. The earth was disturbed, but they covered it with dust."

We step back to let the defusing team do their magic. But there's no bomb. Just a canvas bag full of American uniforms that gets us all scratching our heads.

"What the heck is this about?"

"Whatever it is, it can't be good. We need to get whoever hid them to find out. Bring the K-9s."

We sniff the uniforms, then Rambo and I start tracking,

shoulder to shoulder. Lovely follows, her short legs moving at double speed.

"Wait for me!"

Are you kidding? We ignore her as we try to outrun each other, but we're still shoulder to shoulder when we reach the village.

The locals stare at us with dread as soldiers line them up for me to sniff them. I move from one to the other, looking for the scent I tracked, while Rambo keeps an eye on the lot to make sure they behave.

They all reek like hate and fear, but that's not what I'm looking for. I look for those who left their scent on the uniforms. Like this dude whose fists are so tight, his knuckles turned white. If eyes could kill, I'd be a dead Malinois. But they can't, so I point him out. Next is a white-haired elder with an unkempt beard, then a kid barely taller than me.

My job here is done. I watch the soldiers take them away.

"Mind if I take a sniff?" Rambo asks.

My hackles rise.

"Suit yourself," I growl.

He sniffs one man after another and points out a short skinny kid whose shalwars drag on the ground.

Seriously? I sniff him, and I'd bet my tail against a second-hand bone that he didn't touch those uniforms. Rambo lost it, I think, when I notice the kid's American combat boots.

I'm mortified. My ears go flat, and my tail hides between my legs as we head to base. Technically, I was correct. The kid's scent was not on those uniforms. But practically, I ignored an essential clue and missed a suspect. If it weren't for Rambo, that kid would be free.

That night I lie in my crate with my nose on my paws, wondering if I'm too old for my job.

39

The following day I act like those boots never happened. And, thank Dog, they're all too excited to pay attention to me.

"The new K-9s arrive today," the lieutenant says.

My jaw drops.

Really? New K-9s again? We just got Rambo and Ash, and now we get another team? We've never had four K-9s at the base. I wonder if that means they're getting rid of me. I'd love to know, but

I'm too proud to ask. And what on earth would I say? "Did you get them because I'm a loser?"

So I spend the day shaking on my paws as everyone looks forward to meeting the newcomers.

"Who are they?" Lovely asks.

Brown shrugs.

"Dunno. I think they're new. Never heard those names before. Like Chantix or something. But we're about to find out, aren't we? And what difference does it make, anyhow?"

Good question. What difference does it make? I don't know many active K-9s. All those I knew — Jinx, Butter, Guinness, Fury — they'll never return. I'm the last one left. And not for long, I bet.

"I hope it's a Labrador," Lovely says. "They are the nicest dogs on earth."

I give her the stink eye. I saved her life, and that counts for nothing? Rambo wags his tail left.

"What does that say about Viper and me?"

Lovely is so embarrassed she yawns.

"Sorry, guys. You're both wonderful. I was just thinking about Butter. I hope whoever comes will be as nice as her, that's all."

We go about our day, as usual, and by the time we hear the gates open to let in the growling truck, I'm too exhausted to care. Between yesterday's SNAFU, my unslept night, and the incoming team, I'm spent.

They all file to the gates to meet the newcomers. I stay behind and consider a nap, but that would be rude, so I drag myself to follow.

By the time I reach the truck, Lovely and Rambo are already speaking to a shaggy yellow dog with droopy ears who's got to be a retriever. I may as well be done with this, so I force myself to meet him.

He's too busy bonding with Lovely and Rambo to notice me. But when he does, he jumps back, and his eyes pop out.

"Jinx? Is that you?"

Lovely and Rambo stare at him like he's lost it. I'm stunned. Meeting someone who knew Jinx turns my heart inside out.

I manage to wag my tail.

"Name's Viper. And you?"

"Sorry, Viper. For a moment, I thought I saw a ghost. I'm Prozac, your new mate."

He turns around to offer his butt, and I take my time checking him out. He's not as young as he looks. He's been places and done things, and this long trip took a lot out of him.

I let him sniff my butt, and he takes forever. Nobody has checked me that thoroughly since the Army procurers who selected Jinx and me to join the Army. They didn't sniff our butts, of course, since they were humans. The military isn't bright enough to employ K-9s for that job. But they poked, prodded, and checked every inch of me, even those that aren't on display.

Prozac comes to sniff my nose, and I smell his sorrow.

"You're Jinx's twin."

It's not a question; it's a statement. My heart burns raw with losing Jinx like it happened yesterday.

"I am. And you?"

"I was his best friend. We worked together, trained together, and shared things we couldn't share with anyone else. He told me all about you. He was so proud of you for finding IEDs in the Middle East, but he missed you terribly. He told me so much about you that I feel like I've known you forever."

"What did he tell you?"

"He told me you're brave, sharp, and relentless. He told me you can't quit, and you'll push yourself to the end, no matter what. He hoped to be as good as you someday."

I choke. I always thought Jinx was better than me, and I still do. Oh, how I miss him!

"Do you know what happened to him?"

"Don't you?"

"I know the official line, but not the details. They said Jinx attacked his handler, but I never understood why."

"The man killed Turbo, Jinx's cat. He ran over him with his truck."

"Yep. But..."

"But what?"

"It was an accident. The man didn't mean to hurt that cat."

"Maybe not. But he was drunk. He had no business driving."

40

When the lieutenant comes to see me the next day, his eyes avoid mine.

"Good job on finding those uniforms, Viper. We all know that we can always rely on you."

He doesn't mention the boots, and I'm grateful. Everyone knows it anyhow.

"I have great news for you."

He looks away, and I know he's lying.

"After seven years of service, you are finally ready to retire."

"I am what?"

"You're going home, Viper. Thank you for your lifetime of service. We are proud to have served with you."

I cock my head to understand as the men gather around us, clapping.

"Thank you for your service, Viper."

"You so do deserve to retire."

"Our old Viper's going home."

I'm going home? What home? I have no home other than the base. My tattered gray crate has been my only home ever since George retired, and that's too long ago to count.

The lieutenant leans over to hang a dark tag with a brown and blue ribbon around my neck. There seems to be something written on it, but I can't read.

"I am honored to present you with the PDSA Dickin Medal for Gallantry and Devotion to Duty for your extraordinary service. The Dickin Medal, also known as "The Animal Victoria Cross," was inaugurated in 1943 to honor the work of animals in war. It's been awarded to thirty-four dogs, thirty-two messenger pigeons, four horses, and o cat."

My ears flatten.

"A cat? You're going to give me a medal they gave a cat and a bunch of pigeons?"

"Simon was no ordinary cat. He served on *HMS Amethyst*, and he disposed of many rats, even after being wounded by a blast. His behavior was of the highest order. And the pigeon GI Joe flew twenty miles in twenty minutes to save a hundred Allied Soldiers from being bombed by their own planes. As for Warrior, a horse in World War I...."

My hackles go up. Like really? I need a pigeon medal like I need a catnip refill.

"Where am I going?"

The lieutenant sighs.

"Good question. You know, Viper, we do our best to retire our K-9s with their old trainers. When that's not possible, we look for volunteers to adopt them. But that's not easy. Our K-9 veterans are not pets. After fighting the war, many have trouble adjusting to family life, especially in homes with young children or cats. That's why all the families who adopt K-9s have to be thoroughly vetted. Still, some K-9s can't adjust to living in a civilian home. But you're lucky."

"I am?"

"Dick's family wants to adopt you. His wife hopes you'll bring them comfort."

WHAT? Dick's family? You've got to be kidding! I don't know

those humans, and I don't want to. Dick was the worst human I ever knew, and I want nothing to do with his family.

"How about Sabrina? Or George?"

The lieutenant shakes his head.

"Sorry, I don't know where they are. But I'm sure you'll be happy in Dick's home."

I'm not so sure, and I'd rather not find out. But nobody asked me.

I've served in the army since I was a pup. Seven years of breathing dust, braving the heat, eating MREs, and following orders. Seven years of getting shot at and dodging bombs. Seven years of living to serve. And now they're ditching me like I'm a second-hand bone. That's what my service was worth. That, and a cat medal.

That night I lie with my nose on my paws, remembering Guinness.

"There's more to life than work, Viper. Someday you'll find out."

41

As they load me in the truck, I catch a last glimpse of Lovely's tail waving goodbye, and I've never felt more hopeless. Not even when I found out about Jinx's death. Then, I was too angry to be sad. Now I'm spent.

Lovely tried hard to give me hope.

"You'll be all right, Viper. Just because Dick was Dick doesn't mean his family is the same. They may be lovely humans. They must be if they asked to adopt you, though they never met you. And it's great to have kids in the house."

I cock my head, wondering if she's lost her mind.

"Kids? Great? Are you nuts?"

"Not at all. Brown's kids, Aleta and BB, are lots of fun. And, wherever there are kids, there's food. Lots of food. I don't mean kibble. I mean fries, and ice cream and hot dogs and cookies. Real junk food. And the kids? Even Butter loves them!"

I snort.

"Butter! Butter loves everybody! She doesn't know how not to love! She doesn't have a hateful bone in her body."

"Viper baby, you don't know Butter as well as you think you do. She's way more discerning than that. Go ask Brown if you don't believe me. Either way, she loves the kids and wouldn't trade them for the world. You'll love yours too."

No self-respecting K-9 could ever love kids. She's just trying to make me feel better. I just wish it worked.

Lovely licks my nose one last time and steps aside to let Rambo say goodbye.

"Good luck, Viper. I was honored to work with you. I hope your retirement is everything you hope for and more."

He doesn't know it, of course, but I hoped to never retire. I don't know what to do with myself without work. But I don't have a choice.

"Thanks, Rambo. I'm glad I met you. Do me a favor, please? Look after Lovely. She's young and vulnerable, and she has a lot to learn."

Rambo glances at Lovely, who's chatting with Prozac, and wags his tail.

"Of course. I'll always have my partners' back. But you don't need to worry about her. She may be young and cute, but she's got the best nose on the base, and she's as crafty as a honey badger. That K-9 is anything but vulnerable."

He steps aside to make room for Prozac. He hunches with his ears hanging low, and his eyes show he's hurting. But why? We only just met. Why would he care? But he does. I smell it, and I see it in his eyes.

"Goodbye, Viper. I'm so sorry we didn't have more time together. I miss Jinx like he was my brother, and I know you do too. When I met you, I felt like I got him back. But it wasn't meant to be. I'm sorry we didn't get to share our memories and be friends."

He wags his tail goodbye, and I drown in sadness. Yet another joy the army stole from me. Prozac and I could have talked about Jinx, about life, and grown to be friends and fill each other's void. But they'll ship me out today, and I'll never be back.

"Thanks, Prozac. And thank you for telling me about Jinx. All these years, I tried to understand what happened. Now I do, and

I'm grateful. Take care of yourself, will you? We aren't young anymore. Don't be stupid like me."

Prozac shakes his head.

"Jinx would be so proud of you, Viper. I hope he sees you from wherever he's at and gets to brag to his friends about his hero brother. Until we meet again, my friend."

I don't feel like a hero. I feel like a useless old dog. I'm leaving my home, my work, and my friends to live with the family of the only human I ever hated. I'd rather be with Jinx and with Fury, wherever they are. But this isn't Prozac's fault.

"Thanks, my friend. See you on the other side."

The truck takes off, and I catch the last glimpse of my buddies' sad eyes and droopy ears before the dust drowns them and leaves me alone with my thoughts.

I remember what Guinness said about home.

"Home is where you let your guard down. You can fall asleep on your back if you want. You don't have to worry because everyone loves you, and you're safe."

Wherever I'm going, it won't be like that. I'll never, ever sleep on my back. And I know better than to trust those humans.

42

When the engines stop, my ears start ringing. It's been so long that I can't remember what silence sounds like. I feel like I was born in this crate. But I'm back on the ground, and someone better let me out before I explode.

I've been locked in since the truck in Kandahar rattled my brains through miles and miles of dusty roads. Still locked as I shivered in the dark on the plane, trying to chew my way out of jail. But I couldn't, so I chewed my ball into smithereens. That's the one thing that kept me sane, and I'm grateful to Rambo for dropping it in my crate as I left.

"You'll be all right, Viper. You're the Malligator. If anyone can do it, you can. I can't wait to meet you again."

He dropped his red Kong in my crate as a gift. It couldn't be easy since our balls are precious to us. They keep us going through our training.

The kid's all right, but for being uglier than a jackal. But he grows on you.

I lie in my crate at the special luggage counter, waiting for someone to come, but nobody does. Did they forget? My bladder's ready to pop, and everything inside me hurts. I'm about to embarrass myself when a large woman with dark greasy hair kneels by the grate and stares at me. She smells of meatloaf, detergent, and worry.

"Viper?"

"Who else?"

"I'm Charity, Dick's wife. I'm glad you made it. I'm sorry I'm late, but I had trouble finding someone to look after the kids. Let's go."

Two men load me in a pick-up truck, and off we go. There goes my bladder, I think. But I forget about it as I stick my nose through the bars to breathe the scent of mowed grass and moist earth. It's raining, so I hold out my parched tongue to catch a few drops. It's the first rain I've seen in years, and I love it. There's nothing better than rain — except mud and snow — but there won't be any snow here. Everything's green — the trees, the bushes, the grass. It smells like summer, and this lawn would get a piss out of an old guy with a swollen prostate, I think, as the truck stops by a blue doublewide with black shutters.

Charity opens the crate, and I tumble out. I let go of my bladder, and it's heaven. It takes me forever, but Charity looks away to give me privacy. Like I care!

When I'm done, I sniff the mailbox, then the bushes, and the fence. What a useless little thing! This is nothing like our base fence with its razor-wire topping. This is just a silly white fence with no excuse to exist. I could leap over it with a paw tied behind my back, and I bet even Lovely could clear it. And it doesn't even have a gate.

That throws me off. Seriously? What's the point of a fence without a gate?

"Why do you have a fence without a gate?"

Charity smiles.

"It's nice, isn't it? I always wanted a white picket fence."

"But what's the point if you don't have a gate?"

"Dick painted it only last year."

She doesn't understand me. She's clearly one of the humans

who don't speak dog. Some do, some don't. That doesn't make them bad people, but it makes it hard to communicate.

"Let's go meet the kids, shall we?"

"Do I have to?"

She opens the door to let me in. Dick's home smells just like her: meatloaf and detergent. And kids. Lots of kids.

I step in, and they ambush me. I struggle to keep my teeth to myself.

"There they are: Dick, Carl, and Harry."

Dick, the oldest, is his father's spitting image: blue eyes, straight back, cocky attitude. The other two are dark, sturdy, and submissive.

"Kids, this is Viper, Father's partner. Viper fought alongside your father until the day he died. He got wounded as he tried to save your father's life. We are so lucky that the army allowed us to adopt him, aren't we, kids?"

The young ones nod, but Dick stares at me.

"What happened to my dad?"

Unlike his mother, he speaks dog. I'd rather he didn't, but I do my best to answer.

"Your father got killed on a mission. He was a brave man and did his best, but he had a bad day."

The kid's eyes fill with tears. He's old enough to hurt, but the other two are too young. They hug me, mount me, and touch me everywhere. I hate it. I'd rather be in the desert sniffing bombs or even manning the freaking checkpoint. But I'm not.

Thanks to the army, I'm here. So I lie there as they comb their fingers through my tail and taste my toes, telling myself that killing them is not an option.

It feels like forever before Charity puts them to bed. I curl in a corner, hoping for a peaceful night, but it's not over yet.

"Oh, how I wish I could speak to you, Viper. I'd love to hear about Dick, his last days, and his sacrifice to our country," Charity says.

"No, you wouldn't," I growl.

Fortunately, she doesn't get it. But young Dick does.

"What do you mean?"

Boy, do I wish I'd kept my mouth shut.

"Your mother doesn't want to know what happened to your father. It wouldn't bring her any joy."

"How about me?"

"You neither. You want to remember the man you knew."

Dick's hard eyes look into my soul. He doesn't like me and doesn't trust me. I wonder why.

I wag my tail.

"I never lie."

He stares at me, trying to read my thoughts, then turns to his mother:

"Mother, why don't we let Viper rest? He had a long trip. You go to bed. I'll take him out, then tuck him in for the night."

43

The rain's soft touch softens my heart. I can't remember the last time I was outside without sniffing for IEDs. I breathe in the moist wind, delight in the soft lawn cuddling my paws, and study the memos on the mailbox post.

It's incredible. There's a whole bunch of dogs I never met who live their entire lives without going to war. They eat food that needs no rehydrating, and they have homes and humans that belong to them instead of getting shuffled from one handler to the next. I bet some of them don't even have jobs.

That, to me, is unthinkable since all I know is my job. I sniff and sniff, reading one message after another, and I can't get enough.

Young Dick can't wait any longer.

"What did Father do?"

He's just a kid, barely taller than me. He deserves better than finding out what a small man his father was. He "forgot" to feed me, "forgot" to let me out, "forgot" he had a family when he got Sabrina pregnant, and then "forgot" it was his fault. Even his death was his fault. He was so obsessed with hating Brown that he ignored my warnings until it was too late. There may be worse soldiers out there, but I don't want to meet them.

But this isn't the kid's fault. Thinking his father was a hero will help him cope with his loss. I wish I could tell him that Dick was a wonderful man, but I can't. I never lie, and I'm not about to start now. So I look him in the eye and wag my tail.

"You don't want to know."

"I do."

I yawn.

"You don't. Your dad was your dad when he was here. He loved you and your brothers, and he cared about your mom. War is hell. It does bad things to dogs and to humans. Whatever happened in Kandahar has nothing to do with you. It won't help you, and you don't want to know."

But Dick doesn't believe me. I wish I could help him, but I'm exhausted.

"I'm sorry, Dick. I've had a long day. I have to go."

My bed is an old sweater that smells like Dick, but I'm too tired to care. He's been dead long enough that I've stopped hating him, so I sleep like a log.

The air is clean and crisp, and the grass soft and fragrant as I take my morning walk. Just out of habit, I sniff for IEDs, but there aren't any. Just moist earth, grass, and a few silly squirrels. Cold raindrops fall on me, and I love them.

But I hate being caught in a lie. Dick is a hero to his family. That brings them solace and helps them through their loss. Every day, they ask me about him, and I do my best not to hurt them.

"He was wonderful, wasn't he? He was big and strong and brave," Carl says.

"And handsome," his mother adds.

"He had blue eyes and a straight back," I say.

That's good enough for all of them but Dick. He's torn between wanting to know more and being afraid of it. He's as wary of me as I was of the Afghans.

We continue this terrible truce that makes me feel like an imposter until the day the doorbell rings.

"Open the door," Charity shouts from the kitchen.

Something stirs in the air. My skin tingles, my throat tightens, and I just know my life is about to change.

Dick opens the door to a blimp of a woman who leans back to balance the weight of her belly. I catch a whiff of her, and my heart skips a beat.

This is not a woman — this is Sabrina! I bark with joy and jump to lick her face. She cries and hugs me.

"Viper!"

"Sabrina!"

"I found you! I really found you!"

She hugs me again, and her hair makes me sneeze. She laughs and cries, and I lick off her tears, then I smell her butt to see how she's doing.

Wow! She smells like no other human I've ever sniffed, and she looks like she swallowed a refrigerator. Something's terribly wrong, and I'm worried about her.

"Are you OK?"

"Yep, Viper. Much better now that I found you. How're you doing, my friend?"

"Fair to middling. How did you get so fat?"

I bite my tongue, but it's too late. I flatten my ears in embarrassment, but Sabrina laughs.

"I'm not fat; I'm pregnant. But you wouldn't know the difference, would you?"

"Sorry. Never been pregnant."

She hugs me again, then turns to young Dick, who watches us like a hawk. Her breath catches in her throat as she sees how much he resembles his father.

"Hi. I'm Sabrina. I used to be Viper's handler, and I worked with your father. I'm sorry about your loss."

He nods.

"Let me get my mother."

44

Sabrina keeps her arms around me as we wait for Charity, and I don't mind her being so close. She's always been touchy-feely. I used to find that embarrassing in camp, but now I love her closeness.

"How did you know I was here?"

"Brown emailed me. Lovely harassed him into breaking the rules."

I spare a moment of gratitude to Brown's breaking the rules and to Lovely.

"I heard you had a thing for her. Is she pretty?"

I'd blush if I knew how.

"She's Lovely," I say, as Charity comes to meet us.

She's had a rough night with the baby. Her eyes are red, and she's sweaty and tired, but she smiles as she shakes Sabrina's hand. I bet she wouldn't if she knew where Sabrina's belly comes from.

"Good to see you. We're happy to welcome Viper's friends. And Dick's. I understand you worked together?"

Sabrina's eyes move from Charity's messy hair to her cracked hands.

"Yes. I worked with Viper when Dick worked with Fury. Then I... had a medical issue and returned home. Dick was kind enough to take on Viper and work with him, even though he already had Fury."

Sabrina bites her lip. It's hard to pretend that Dick was anything but an ice-hole, but she does her best.

"Thanks for coming. We all cherish Dick's memory, and we'd love to learn more. Is there anything you could share with us?"

Sabrina stares at the kids, and they stare back. She sighs.

"Fury was a lovely K-9. He was smart, handsome, and dedicated, just like his older sister Guinness. I worked with her too. What a great K-9 she was. After she left, it was wonderful to work with Fury. You couldn't hope for a better K-9."

Young Dick's face twists with pain. For the first time, I realize that Fury was his puppy. How thick I am! Young Dick and Fury grew up together. The kid must have loved Fury and mourned his loss. Oh, how I wish I'd thought about this before. I could talk about Fury for weeks and have nothing but good things to say!

Sabrina wipes her eyes.

"Dick was a remarkable man. He was good-looking, smart, and such a charmer. I've never met anyone like him."

So far, she's stuck to the truth, but I can see her struggling to say something nice about Dick.

"There was this one time. We were on a mission. Viper and I were in the lead while Dick and Fury brought up the rear. Viper sniffed for IEDs, and I watched his back. We were close to our target when Viper smelled the enemy. We took off after them, and we were both so busy that we overlooked the sharpshooters who waited for us. Fury and Dick saw them and told us to take cover. We dropped to the ground just as the bullets flew over our heads. We'd both be dead if it weren't for them."

That's not entirely true, but it's close. Fury called, and I took cover. I don't know what Dick was doing — checking his boogers or taking a selfie. But it's close enough to not be an outright lie.

The kids stare at us with eyes as big as saucers. Charity wipes her eyes and grabs Sabrina's hand.

"Thank you for sharing this with us. This gives me solace, and I know it helps the kids too. Thank you so much for coming to tell us about Dick."

Sabrina sighs.

She wants her hand back — she can't love the touch of Dick's wife — but puts up with it for as long as she can. Then her dark eyes catch mine, and I can smell she's ready.

"Thank you, Charity. I'm glad to meet Fury and Dick's family. I'm sorry for your loss, and I'm inspired by your bravery. But I didn't come to tell you about Dick. I came to take Viper home.

45

Time freezes. The house is so quiet, you could hear a flea sneeze.

Charity drops Sabrina's hand.

"I'm sorry. You said...."

"I came to take Viper home."

The air is thick with apprehension. Sabrina dropped a bomb in Charity's lap. She has to deal with it, but she's vulnerable and unprepared. She didn't plan for this.

Sabrina did.

"Viper was my partner, and he's my best friend. I need him in my life, and he needs me too. I appreciate your caring for him, but he only spent a few weeks with Dick. Viper belongs with me."

Charity's eyes grow wide as she stares at Sabrina.

"But... But Viper was Dick's partner. He was with him until the very end and tried to save his life. That's what they said when they offered Viper to us for adoption. They said the kids were too young, but they made an exception."

Sabrina sighed.

"I understand. I appreciate your caring for Viper, and I know he does too. But Viper belongs with me."

"But he's been here for weeks. And he adjusted so well! And

we're going to do the best for him. He's is the only link to Dick we have left. We can't let him go!"

"If you want to do what's best for him, let him come with me."

Charity's troubled eyes look from Sabrina to the kids, then to me.

"But he loves it here, don't you, Viper? Don't you want to stay with us?"

I yawn like I always do when I'm stressed. I wish I could say something that wouldn't hurt her, but nothing comes to mind.

"I..."

Sabrina sighs like she's ready to jump in cold water. She's about to explain where her swollen belly comes from. She'll tell them that Dick betrayed them, and she'll destroy his memory to take me away. But these people don't deserve it. They've suffered enough.

I cock my head.

"Are you really going to do that?"

She glares at me.

"Are you kidding? I'd kill him right here and now if he weren't dead already. I'm sorry for them, but I won't let you go. I'll do whatever it takes. You are my family and my best friend. I'd lie and steal to get you back. Telling the truth is easy."

"It will hurt them."

"I'm sorry. But it's not our fault. We didn't do this; Dick did. I'd love to spare them the pain, but we both know the truth."

"I wish we didn't have to hurt Charity and the kids."

"Me too."

We're so busy talking that we forgot about young Dick.

"How well did you know my father?" he asks Sabrina.

"I knew him very well."

His eyes shine with tears as he turns to his mother.

"Mother?"

"Yes?"

"Viper belongs with Sabrina. She's been his handler for way

longer than Father was. She needs him to look after her. We must let him go."

Charity stares at him like he's lost it. He's only trying to protect her, but she doesn't know.

"Are you serious?"

"Yes."

"But why?"

"You don't want to know," he says, glancing at Sabrina's belly.

46

Guinness was right. Home is where you can sleep on your back and never worry because you're with those you love and trust.

I'm finally home. Sabrina and I go for long walks without looking for IEDs. We play with my new ball and watch TV in the evenings. Well, Sabrina does. I watch her and the squirrels, and I let her know when someone passes by, especially if they're cats.

It's just the two of us, and I wouldn't want it any other way. Sabrina smells happy and content, though she gets bigger every day. I'm worried she'll no longer fit in the car. She's already tight behind the wheel. But other than that, life couldn't be better.

Until one night when she wakes me up with her screams. I jump to check on things, but nothing smells amiss. She had a nightmare, I think. But then she yells again.

I go to wake her up, but she's wide awake.

"Are you OK?"

"I think it's time."

She tries to sit up but falls back, clutching her belly.

"Time for what?"

"Time for the baby."

Oops. I forgot about the baby — sort of. I didn't really, but life was just fine the way it was, so I ignored it. You know, like when your tail is dirty, but you're too busy talking to your friends to clean it?

"Viper, I have to go. Be a good boy. I'll be back soon."

I tried to follow her, but the ambulance people wouldn't let me.

So I sat by the window and watched them take her away, wondering if she'd ever return.

They seldom do. That's what happened to Butter and Guinness. And even Sabrina. The ambulance took them, and they never came back.

What if Sabrina doesn't return?

I'll just wait until she does. When she comes back, I'll be here.

But what if she never does? Like Andrew?

Sabrina isn't Andrew. She'll come back for me.

But what if she doesn't?

Then I'll just have to wait forever. Like Hachiko, that Akita who went to the train station every day to wait for his human who never returned.

I lay by the dining room window where I can watch the whole driveway and start waiting.

The sun comes up.

The sun goes down.

What if she returns with a kid? Young Dick wasn't bad, but the other two were terrors. Sabrina's kid may be even worse. What if it pulls my tail and sticks its fingers in my ears? Phew! But maybe she won't bring it home. She might just leave it there. I hope.

I lay by the window, waiting.

The sun comes up.

The sun goes down.

The sun comes up again.

It feels like forever.

I'm still waiting when a car pulls in the driveway, and Sabrina comes out. Her belly shrunk, but she's got a package decked with pink ribbons. My heart sinks. Is that the kid?

The door opens, and I rush to meet her. She puts down the package to hug me and rub my ears.

"So good to see you, Viper. Were you a good boy?"

"Of course. Other than eating the dish sponge and the soap. The socks don't count; they were dirty anyhow. How about you?"

"Look what I brought you. This is your sister."

My sister? Really?

I'm flooded with hope. Is she like Jinx?

I check her out. Phew! This is no Jinx! It's soft, pink, and smaller than a cat. It has brown fuzz on its head, and it smells like milk.

"My sister? Really?"

"Yes."

I sniff it again, and it opens its eyes the color of a stormy sky and furrows its brow to stare at me. My heart melts. I've never seen something prettier. Not even Lovely.

"Her name is Ava."

"Ava? What sort of name is that? What does it mean?"

"It doesn't mean anything. It's just her name."

"Names have to mean something. Like Butter or Guinness or Viper."

"So, what would you call her?"

I sniff her again.

"Let's call her Poop."

AFTERWORD

Thanks for reading K-9 VIPER, The Veteran's Story. I hope you enjoyed it. If you did, please take a minute to leave a review and tell a friend to help others find this book. I'd appreciate it.

And don't miss the rest of the K-9 Heroes series. If you enjoyed Viper, you'd like them too.

Check out Becoming K-9, Book #1 in the K-9 Heroes series, and Bionic Butter, Book #2.

Lovely K-9, Book #4 is now on preorder.

Visit RadaJones.com to sign up for updates, get freebies and stay in touch. I love hearing from you!

Rada

K-9 HEROES

ABOUT THE AUTHOR

Born in Transylvania, just ten miles from Dracula's Castle, Rada grew up between communists and vampires. That taught her that humans are fickle, but one can always trust dogs and books. So, she read everything, from food wrappers to the phone book (too many characters, too little action), and adopted every stray, from dogs to frogs.

She immigrated to Connecticut to join her husband, then spent years studying medicine and saving lives in the ER. But she still speaks like Dracula's cousin.

She lives with her husband Steve, their German Shepherd Guinness, and their deaf cat Paxil in a tiny mountain cabin. She wakes at 3 AM to write before she hikes, cooks, reads, and plots audacious journeys to dreamy places.

Check out RadaJones.com for updates and freebies, starting with MOM, the story of Guinness's mom. Rada loves hearing from you.

facebook.com/RadaJonesMD
twitter.com/@JonesRada
instagram.com/RadaJonesMD
bookbub.com/profile/rada-jones

ABOUT THIS BOOK

This K-9 memoir is a work of fiction. Dogs don't write much, and they publish even less. They can read our souls, but their spelling is nothing to write home about.

That's why I wrote Viper's story for him. Over years, I've belonged to many dogs who loved me and taught me to talk Dog before abandoning me for the rainbow bridge. Speaking Dog is magic. It's not about twisting your tongue to utter silly sounds. It's about smelling, watching, and feeling each other in your hearts. That's why dogs don't lie. How can you lie when you taste someone's tears, lean against their thigh and feel their heartbeat? There's no room for deception in Dog like there is in human language.

Viper's story is one of courage and devotion. He lived for his mission until, somewhere along the way, he learned there's more to life than work. Like friendship, love, and home. And we're never too old to find them.

This book is my love letter to Viper and all the dogs who make us better people.

Rada

BOOKS BY RADA JONES

BECOMING K-9: A Bomb Dog's Memoir

(K-9 Heroes: Book 1)

BIONIC BUTTER: A Three-Pawed K-9 Hero

(K-9 Heroes: Book 2)

K-9 VIPER: The Veteran's Story

(K-9 Heroes: Book 3)

LOVELY K-9: A Prison Puppy

(K-9 Heroes: Book 4)

OVERDOSE: An ER Phycological Thriller

(ER Crimes: The Steele Files Book 1)

MERCY: An ER Thriller

(ER Crimes: The Steele Files Book 2)

POISON: An ER Thriller

(ER Crimes: The Steele Files Book 3)

STAY AWAY FROM MY ER, and Other Fun Bits of Wisdom

Wobbling Between Humor and Heartbreak

ER CRIMES: The Steele Files

Box Set: Books 1-3

EXCERPT FROM LOVELY K-9

A PRISON PUPPY

The hairy woman glares at me over her round glasses, and I can smell she doesn't like me, though I don't know why.

I did my best to charm her - wagged my tail, barked, even rolled on my back - but nothing helped. If anything, it made it worse. Her thin lips zipped together, and her ears blushed with anger.

Jermain calls me, but I don't have time for him right now. I need to sniff Hairy's privates to figure out her problem. I can tell she's got a bug up her butt.

Jermain insists.

"Springy, come here."

I wag my tail, telling him to wait until I'm done with Hairy. I push to burrow my nose in her crotch, but she pulls away.

She cuts her eyes to Jermain.

"Are you coming to get her, or just stand there screaming like a fool?"

Jermain's brown face darkens with anger. He lumbers over, clips his leash to my collar, and drags me back to his stool. He sits, holding me between his knees.

The silence is so thick you could bite it. My four littermates sit on their butts glued to their humans, who are sweating bullets. Every eye in the rec room is on us.

They all stink of fear, and I wonder why. There's nothing scary here: gray concrete floors reflecting the bright lights, dark green walls broken by numbered doors with barred windows, and Hairy.

"You realize she won't make it if you don't learn to control her, don't you?"

Jermain shrinks.

"Do you or don't you?"

"Yes, ma'am."

"You have a week. If this dog doesn't know at least thirty of her hundred commands by then, she's out. And so are you."

Her gritty voice and pointed finger raise my hackles. I growl to let her know, but she ignores me. I open my mouth to bark, but Jermain's sweaty hands close around my muzzle, keeping me quiet.

Hairy glares at him one more time then turns to the others.

"That applies to you all. None of you is doing as well as you should. This is not a day camp, people. This is a serious business. We are here to train service dogs for our veterans. These dogs will change someone's life – if you train them."

"I chose you five out of a hundred inmates who wanted to redeem themselves. You're all behind bars because of the terrible things you did, and you said you wanted to give back. Then do so."

"Out there, five veterans with PTSD are hoping that one of these dogs will help them reclaim their lives. Your job is to train these dogs to support their human. That's why you teach them to "lap," and "nudge," and "visit." That's why they learn to get help when their human is in trouble. But you first need to teach them the right attitude."

"These dogs aren't here to roam free and have fun. They are here to focus on their human. Their life must revolve around their human. If you can't make them do that, the rest doesn't matter. You've failed your mission, and you've failed your dog too."

She glares at us one more time, then grabs her bag and storms out. The building shudders as the heavy door slams.

The inmates stare at each other, then at the graying warden watching them. He sighs.

"She's right, you know. That woman may be loud and obnoxious, but she's right. And she'll do like she said. You know how many dogs graduated last time?"

The men shake their heads.

"Three. Out of six. Half didn't make it."

The silence is so heavy it hurts.

"What happened to the other three?" Jermain asks.

The warden shakes his head.

"That's the wrong question, Jermain. You should ask what happened to the inmates? They went back to the general population and will never get another chance to train a puppy. More importantly, what happened to the three veterans who waited for those dogs to wake them from their nightmares, help them walk down the street, and have someone to talk to? They didn't get them. And if you folks don't get your act together, they won't get them this time either."

The smell of fear turns into dejection and shame. The men drag themselves out with their heads hanging. The dogs follow them with flattened ears. Jermain and I are last.

I know this is my fault, even though I don't know why, so I hide my tail between my legs as I follow Jermain to the door.

The warden calls.

"Jermain?"

"Yes, sir."

"You're a lifer, but I still recommended you for this program. I didn't expect you to disappoint me."

Jermain hangs his head.

"I'm sorry, sir."

"Sorry is not good enough. Are you going to train this dog, or are you just wasting our time? And hers. You know damn well that the first few months in a puppy's life are essential, but you already wasted weeks and weeks. Soon enough, she'll be too old to learn. Are you going to do what it takes?"

"Yes, sir, I will."

"You will what?"

"I will make her into an obedient dog."

I cock my head.

What's obedient?

Buy LOVELY K-9: A Prison Puppy

EXCERPT FROM BIONIC BUTTER

A THREE-PAWED K-9 HERO

The kennel smells sick. Dozens of dogs, some big, some small, some purebreds, some mutts, all reeking of pain and worry as they struggle to unwrap their bandages and shake off their cones of shame. And most of them are K-9s.

How do I know? By the smell. K-9s come in all sizes, shapes, and colors, but we all live for the job. We can smell that on each other like humans can smell perfume.

"How ya doing, girl?"

I struggle to lift my head. A white pit bull with one black eye sniffs at me across from my cell, wagging his hot-dog tail like crazy. He looks just like the dog in the Target commercial, and he grins from his black ear to the white one, despite his cone of shame and the bandages around his leg and chest.

I wag my tail—sort of.

"Fair to middling. You?"

"I'm good, thanks. So good to meet you! I can't wait for breakfast."

His short tail quivers with excitement as he dances on his feet, even the one that's in a cast. He's the happiest K-9 I've ever seen, so much so that I start to wonder if he is a K-9 at all. We, K-9s, are all sorts of wonderful, but happy is not at the top of the list.

He points his nose toward me and sniffs until the dust from the floor makes him sneeze. I know he'd love to get properly introduced and smell my butt, but we're too far apart.

"What's your name, lovely lady?"

"Butter. I'm K-9 Corporal Butter. You?"

"I'm Target."

No kidding.

"Are you a K-9?"

"Of course. I am a qualified customs agricultural agent. I work for the TSA, where I sniff for smuggled agrarian products. Say somebody tries to smuggle in lemons from Sicily or oranges from Costa Rica. Unless properly inspected, they may bring in diseases or aphids that could destroy our crops. My job is to find them and stop them. I also sniff for contraband animals. My sister Raisin works in the field too, but she specializes in Coconut Rhinoceros Beetle Larvae. They are the bane of palm trees."

"Wow. I didn't know such a job existed."

"Sure, it does. It's essential, and also lots of fun. I once found a suitcase full of pangolins."

"Penguins?"

"Not even close. Penguins are those fat birds dressed in tuxedoes. Pangolins are small animals wearing scaly armored vests instead of fur. They look funny, like miniature dinosaurs, but they're useful since they eat ants and termites. Sadly, Chinese traditional medicine practitioners believe their scales and meat have healing properties, so they pay big money to get them. Poachers bring them over from Sri Lanka and the Philippines. They pack them like oiled sardines, so most of them don't make it through the trip."

"That's terrible."

"Yes. Especially if you're a pangolin."

I try to imagine being locked in a suitcase with a dozen other dogs, but I can't. Good. I'm already miserable enough. Fortunately, the whole kennel starts barking, so I forget what I was worried about.

"What's going on?"

"They're bringing breakfast."

Breakfast! I try to stand, but my left front paw wants none of it, and I fall on my side as my leg explodes with pain.

Target cocks his blocky head, his nose wrinkled in worry.

"Are you OK?"

"Middling. You?"

"What happened to you?"

"I was on a mission. Then I got here."

"How?"

"I don't know. How about you?"

He looks down, his ears flat with embarrassment.

"I... I was stupid."

"What did you do?"

"My handler and I were going home after our shift."

"And?"

"I saw a cat."

"Yes?"

"I... I was a bad dog. I took off after it, and I got hit by a car."

"I'm so sorry, Target. That's terrible!"

"Terribly stupid. But enough about me. What happened to you?"

That's so unusual it makes me wonder if Target is really a male. He smells like one, but he's so caring you'd think he's female. Most males seldom remember to ask you how you're doing, and they never do it twice.

"I don't know."

I try to remember. We went on patrol. We were searching for explosives in the village near our base. I was leading the team inside the wire, then...

"I got shot."

"Where?"

"In Kandahar."

"No. Where in your body?"

"I don't know."

"What hurts?"

"Everything."

"What hurts the most?"

"My front paw."

"Do you still have it?"

What a silly question. Of course, I do. It's right there, bandaged, painful, and useless as it is. I can't stand on it or even lick it, but it's there.

"Sure."

"Good. Because some canines lose it, and that's the end of their K-9 career."

"Really?"

"Yep. Does it hurt?"

"Like a son of a gun."

"That's great. It's bad news if it stops hurting."

"Why?"

"Because it's like with us. When you stop hurting, you're dead."

Buy BIONIC BUTTER: A Three-Pawed Hero

CPSIA information can be obtained
at www.ICGtesting.com
Printed in the USA
LVHW081550200223
739935LV00029B/469